THE NOVELLAS

Kealan Patrick Burke

ISBN: 1484803264
ISBN-13: 978-1484803264

THE NOVELLAS

DEDICATION

For Rian, the youngest lemon, bound to be the best lemon in the grove

TABLE OF CONTENTS

THE TENT

THE TENT

Pepper is nervous, and that in turn makes McCabe uneasy. The collie is not given to barking at every sound or she'd long ago have driven him insane. Up here in the mountains, they have long shared real estate with rabbits, cows, deer and sheep, and birds aplenty. Pepper learned this as a pup, learned to recognize the ambient sounds of the mountain's many residents, and now rarely does she raise her head from her tattered old wicker basket in the corner of the cabin.

Tonight, however, her head and her hackles are raised. Her brown eyes are wide and wet and fixed on the door of his small bungalow as if trouble casts its shadow on the other side.

Sitting before the fire, the air tinged with smoke, the damp logs still crackling and spitting three hours after he set them alight, McCabe watches the dog watching the door, and cocks his own head in an effort to detect whatever might have upset his old friend. Unsurprisingly, he hears nothing but the wind. Twenty years ago, maybe even ten, he'd have stood a slim chance of competing with the dog's hearing, but not anymore. They are both in the winters of their lives, but Pepper still has the edge on him when it comes to the senses.

Reluctantly he stands, his knees crackling louder than the logs, and puts one rough hand on his lower back, absently massaging away the dull fiery pain that settles in like a cuckoo whenever the weather turns cold. Pepper gives him a brief glance, her worried eyes reflecting the small flames in the hearth, clearly unwilling to break her concentration from whatever has her dander up, and goes back to watching the door.

"What is it, Pep?" he asks in a soothing voice. "What's got you upset?"

The dog whines but does not look at him.

Visitors are rare during the day, and rarer still at night. When anyone does have occasion to seek his cabin out, it is seldom with good news.

As he shrugs on his peacoat and sighs, Pepper gingerly steps from her basket and plods over to join him. She trembles slightly and McCabe doesn't like that at all. She may be old, but he has always thought of her as fearless. He reaches down and he is alarmed when the dog lowers her head as if afraid she is about to be struck, something he has never done in all their years together.

He frowns. "This is one of those times I wish you could talk," he says, something he has wished often in the four years since his wife Susan passed away.

Coat fastened, he fetches his old hand-carved, bleached pine walking stick from the corner by the door and turns his attention back to the dog.

Her head is still bowed in deference to the unknown threat. As he watches her tremble, he briefly considers abandoning the idea of venturing out into the cold and giving Trooper Lyons a call instead. Then he just as quickly dismisses the notion. Lyons is a good and fair man, but he's also a drunk and as it's after ten on a Wednesday night, the chances of finding him sober are slim. He'd undoubtedly balk at the idea of the twenty mile drive to the mountain, especially to investigate what will no doubt prove to be little more than the result of a nervous dog's hypersensitivity. Instead he'll slur a few reassurances and promise to stop by in the morning. But because McCabe has unwavering faith in his dog's ability to sense something amiss out there, he doesn't fancy the idea of waiting that long. The wondering will keep him awake all night if he doesn't go see what it is.

"How likely am I to run into a demon or a ghost out there, girl?" he asks the dog.

Pepper says nothing, just looks through him to the door as if, merely by mentioning it, he has become a ghost himself.

And though the old man feels silly at the note of fear pealing through him, he can't deny that the dog has him more worried than he's accustomed to being. The last time he saw Pepper this alarmed, McCabe had stood up from the supper table and followed her outside into the fine spring evening, where he found his wife lying prostrate in the yard, her heart as dead and cold as the rocks upon which she lay, her laundry basket turned on its side, the freshly laundered clothes strewn about her head and shoulders.

He doesn't like to think about that now, no more than he likes the waves of terror that radiate from the dog and creep into the marrow of his old bones.

Something is wrong out there, and he tells himself that if he has any sense at all, he'll stay locked up inside with the old girl and wait until sunup to go investigate. But then he reminds himself that people sometimes get themselves in trouble on the mountain; youngsters mostly, sometimes the occasional hiker who tries to scale the peak without doing their homework first. The mountainside is full of bottomless holes and crevasses partially concealed by shrubbery, mires disguised as weed-choked clearings, and loose shale that can go from under you in a heartbeat and send you tumbling. He's watched many a man being airlifted off the slope, fielded questions about youths gone missing, some of whom showed up looking worse for wear, some of whom were never seen again. And every time he'd felt a twinge of guilt for not intervening, for not shooing them off the slope or at least giving them some advice on how best to proceed if they were determined to carry on. He knows it is ridiculous, of course. He can hardly be held responsible for what others choose to do of their own free will, but the fact of the matter is that nobody out here knows the mountain better than he does—he has after all, lived here for the greater part of his long life—and so he feels a sort of guardianship toward both the mountain and the people who traverse its hostile terrain. He is one of the few people who still call the mountain home, the lure of the big city too great to resist and the increasing lack of agricultural viability too great to survive. He knows the mountain is a dangerous place, but he has never really feared it, despite acknowledging that there are things about it that he can't explain and that don't always make sense.

But thanks to Pepper, he fears it now.

"C'mon then," he tells the dog, and tries not to let her anxiety freeze him in place. With one last longing look back at the fire, he sighs, snatches a flashlight from its hook by the door, and opens the door to the night.

It is quiet out there. No birdsong, no bark of mating animals, no shriek of cornered prey. The slope rises greenly up to his left until swathed by a dark bandolier of beech and oak. Boulders speckle the plain around his small cabin, looking like knuckled bones in the cloudy moonlight.

Behind him, Pepper whines on the threshold, the small silver bell on her collar jingling as she reluctantly does her duty and follows her master out the door.

Troubled, he closes the door behind her, offers her a soothing word she does not, despite the acuity of her senses, seem to hear, and heads off toward the only thing on the mountain that has immediately registered as out of place: the small amber glow of a campsite somewhere up there in the trees. He assumes that if there's something amiss, he'll find it there. What he does not yet know is the nature of the trouble, and offers up a silent prayer to his deceased wife that he will not regret answering its call.

* * *

The storm had come upon them without warning, a hungry, violent thing that roared in from the north, as if they'd camped on a railroad track assumed abandoned only to have a freight train barrel through in an explosion of sudden light and noise.

And now their tent was destroyed and they were lost in the dark woods, having fled in the kind of panic unique to unseasoned campers, shelter taking precedence over direction.

"Mike? Do you know where we're going?"

"Sure, babe."

This is the first of many lies he has told her on this trip, and he fears it won't be the last. They're lost, and it's his fault—of course it is, isn't everything?—but Mike is determined not to acknowledge the fact if only to deprive his wife of just one more reason to think less of him.

"You're sure?" Emma yells at him over the wind and rain that sends spectral horses galloping through his flashlight beam.

The verdure weaves and dances around them in submarine

symphony. They are miles from anywhere. There are only trees here, tall and stolid and dark, the forest floor soft and spongy, greedily sucking down the rain and their ill-prepared feet after months of drought. Above their heads, the canopies of the beech, poplar, and oak are thick enough to appear conjoined, relegating the lightning to startlingly bright pulses between the crowded boles.

Mike stops, eager to go on, eager to be out of this interminable forest, but glad for the chance to catch his breath, which a quarter mile or so ago became labored and now feels like he's pulling flaming cotton into his lungs instead of air. The hiking boots he bought just for this occasion are sawing open the backs of his heels, making each step torture. He turns to face his wife and son, knowing they need reassurance, knowing he could use it just as much, and struggles against the encumbrance of the backpack full of items that were of little enough use before the storm and are absolutely useless now, and his yellow slicker, which flaps madly as if eager to be free of him. He empathizes, eager as he is right now to be free of himself and the situation into which he has thrust them. This was a mistake, and probably the last one he'll ever make as a married man. That it was supposed to revitalize their crumbling union is only the larger part of the tragedy this trip has become. That he knew his luck would pull the rug out from under him is another. Because the last time he can remember his poor luck changing to any substantial degree, he was three weeks shy of his thirty-first birthday, still living with his parents, unemployed and flirting with alcoholism as a way to subvert his loneliness, when he answered the door to a perky blonde, her pretty face glowing with rehearsed Republican charm as she espoused the benefits of reelecting George Bush Sr. It had taken uncharacteristic levels of courage and impulsivity for him to ask out a girl he knew was so far out of his league they likely didn't share the same quality of oxygen, but it had to have been pure luck, or some other strange upset in the mechanics of the universe, that had made her response an affirmative one. Luckier still that he hadn't blown it on their subsequent dates, that she hadn't seen—or that she chose to ignore—the insecurity that hounded him like a starving dog he'd been foolish enough to feed and now couldn't shake.

That blonde is not as pretty now, and he knows not all of that can be blamed on the weather. Her red slicker clings to a body made shapeless by the years, the disappointment, and the stress of being married to a man crippled by the ever increasing weight of his own failure and unrealized dreams. Her hair, which has lost its luster and faded in synch with her expectations of him, is pasted to her pallid face, but not enough to hide the doubt from eyes made darker by the shadow of his presence in their marriage.

"I think so, yes," he tells her, and even to his own ears it sounds like a "no". But the lies seem to come easier the deeper into the woods they go, and he doesn't care if they've become as transparent as the rain-horses riding through their flashlight beams. He can see on her face and in her posture as she hugs herself against the relentless battering of the storm that she recognizes the lie, but knows better than to challenge it, especially when she is not the only one who might suffer from its exposure. With a smile of feeble wattage, she turns away from him and drops to her knees on the sodden, steaming carpet of dead leaves. Cody, their thirteen-year-old, who has been trailing them soundlessly and with a complete and enviable absence of worry, finds her face with his flashlight beam.

The boy smiles, and as he looks from his mother's face to the storm-wracked woods around them, Mike sees the twin sparks of wonder in his son's eyes, and feels a tightening in his throat. The boy has a spirit he could not possibly have inherited from his parents, the genesis of his cheerful disposition an equal mystery. Tears prick the corners of Mike's own eyes and he does not bother to sleeve them away. The rain will excuse them.

I don't want to lose my son, he thinks.

Whatever Emma is saying to the boy is lost in a peal of thunder that sounds like the roar of some forest god enraged by their intrusion, and even as Mike winces against the violence of it, he tries to read in Cody's face the impact of Emma's words.

I don't want to lose my boy, he thinks, *don't take him from me*. The dread that lies like a cold hard stone in the pit of his belly is a wicked thing, an ever-present thing, and with it comes an irrational certainty that whatever his wife is saying, it is designed to undermine the child's confidence in his father's ability to see them through this nightmare.

Worse, he knows such speculation may be depressingly close to the mark.

It's time we had a talk about Daddy, he imagines his wife telling their child. *It's time for you to realize the sad truths we've been keeping from you. First of all, we're lost because your father thought taking us into the wilderness would somehow keep us together. But it won't, because I hate him, and in time, you'll learn to hate him too. But don't worry; I plan to get us both away before he can destroy your life like he did Mommy's. That is, if we don't die out here first.*

Cody picks that moment to nod in agreement, compounding Mike's paranoia, and abruptly he is reminded of his own childhood, specifically his mother's habit of turning the volume on the TV down to nothing whenever a character started using foul language, like "damn" or "heck", or discussing subjects she deemed inappropriate, like alcohol, or drugs, or romance. *Not for your ears, Mikey,* she would tell him, and he would wait impatiently for the sound to come back. Sometimes the silence only lasted until the scene changed, or until the commercials. Sometimes his mother would get distracted and forget to turn it back up at all, and he would be sent to bed with a headful of questions about what those characters might have been discussing that was so terrible he'd been forbidden from hearing it. He would learn it all in the schoolyard when the other kids discussed the latest episodes of *Hawaii Five-O* and *Bonanza*, and he would laugh right along, pretending he was one of them, knowing he wasn't. Since then, he has been an outsider, and he is made intrinsically aware of that feeling again now as he stands watching his wife counseling his son in a dire situation of Mike's own making, helpless to do anything but hope he's wrong about the weight of their words.

As the thunder rolls away into the woods to the left of them, Emma touches the boy's cheek and rises. As she approaches Mike, she folds her arms again—a natural reaction to the hostile weather, but also, according to their marriage counselor, a defensive posture, the manifestation of which seems directly proportional to her proximity to her husband. When she reaches him, he sees that she is shivering.

"Is it safe to be out here with all this lightning?"

"It's not like we have a choice," he says. "But we'll be fine."

"Well, whatever the case, we should keep going," she says, a bead of rain suspended from a nose the cold has made red and raw.

He nods. "I think we should be close to the campground offices. Can't be more than ten, twenty minutes from here."

She looks at him for a long moment before speaking again. "What makes you think that?"

It's a question he had hoped she wouldn't ask, because the truth is that he *doesn't* think that, has no idea how far they are from anything except lost. The truth is that he knew an hour ago, right around the time he felt the ground begin to rise ever so slightly upward instead of down, that they had gotten completely turned around. The campground offices were in a small valley between the hills. This much, he remembered. If they were headed the right way, the going would have been easier because they'd have been on a decline. The trees would have thinned out too, but the longer they walk, the denser the woods become. The reality, as terrible as it is, is that, yes, he has them well and truly lost, probably miles away from anyone who might be able to help, and all he's doing now is walking in the hope of finding a cabin, or a lodge, or any kind of shelter.

He knows Emma knows this too, and that the long look she gave him was her way of parting the veil of his deception and looking at the complete truth of the matter for herself. He decides the best thing to do is to change the subject, and what better subject than the one that's hanging over them as heavy as the storm.

"About earlier…" he says.

She shrugs, but does not meet his gaze. "Forget it. You were upset."

"Yeah, but still, I shouldn't have snapped at you. It wasn't your fault. The tent was a cheap piece of crap anyway."

The slight smile is very slight indeed, but more than he hoped for, so it will do just fine for now. "Yeah, it was. I did try to tell you that. Made a better kite than a tent."

The levity, here in this frightening, storm-washed darkness, is so unexpected and so desperately needed, he bursts out laughing. Cody, still enthralled by the hissing, weaving, thunderous woods around them, looks in their direction and smiles. *Such a happy child*, he thinks. *So unflappable. He didn't get that from me.* But in the extensive catalogue of his failures, he's thankful that he can at least count his son as a success, a good thing, the one bright spot in the Rorschach pattern of his uneven life, even if ultimately he cannot find a way to keep them all together.

And yet you didn't want him here. This is yet another unpleasant truth. It isn't that he doesn't love the boy, because he does, more than anything. It was just that he'd wanted to be alone with Emma, to get her out of the quagmire of routine of which their son was an integral part, and to discuss with her the kinds of pressing issues not meant to be spoken aloud around children for fear of shattering their illusion of familial security. That she had insisted on bringing Cody with them gave the impression that she wasn't nearly as enthused at the idea of being alone with him as he'd been. Even his choice of destination had left her nonplussed.

"If you want to take a trip, why don't we go to a resort somewhere and enjoy a little luxury for a while?" she'd said, and even now he can't say why that had rankled so much. Perhaps it was the implication that she had *never* enjoyed luxury with him and would have embraced the opportunity to do so. Either way, it has been a disaster from the start, and nothing that's happened since has improved the quality of the situation. Until now.

Emma's smile has grown, just a bit, but these days that might as well be a brilliant lighthouse beam in the dark, scalding away the shadows, at least for a little while. It gives him hope, however tenuous, that maybe things *can* get better.

"It sure did fly, didn't it?" he says, and pictures their miserable old tent, picked up from the clearance section at their local Wal-Mart for a song. Less than five minutes into the storm, and with the sound of staggered applause, the wind tore it free of the pegs and sent it flying away like a pterodactyl to tangle itself high in the canopy above their heads, where it flapped and twisted and snapped like a creature chastising them for trying to keep it tethered. In retrospect, the image was comical, but at the time, exposed to the sudden shock of the cold rain and biting wind, and yet another goddamn disaster in a year, a *life*, replete with them, his initial reaction had been to blame Emma for not hammering the pegs in deep enough. If he was honest, he still believed that, but if accountability was the game du jour, then he'd already beaten her by a wide margin. She might have lost the tent; he had gotten *them* lost. And considering his fears about the fragility of their marriage, it had been foolish to rebuke her for anything at all.

"Have you checked your phone?" she asks.

"Yeah. I've been keeping it off to save the battery, but I checked it about ten minutes ago. Still no signal. That was kind of the point of coming here, but it sure doesn't help us much in a pinch, does it? How about yours?"

"Left it in the car. Didn't think we'd need it."

The idea of the battered old Toyota (itself so cheap and old, it has contributed to multiple instances of Mike's bad luck) with its shelter and warmth, is like an oasis to Mike. In daylight, he figures it might even be visible from here, but at night, with the storm raging around them, he might as well have parked on the moon.

"What about that compass app thingy you downloaded for Cody?"

"It would need to know our location via the GPS," he says. "And if we had the GPS, we'd have the location, and we wouldn't be lost." As the words leave his mouth on a cloud of staggered vapor, he realizes they represent the first honest answer to the question she asked in the beginning, and his smile fades. "I'm sorry," he says, wincing as a fresh gust of wind sprays rain into their faces. "I messed up."

She chooses not to acknowledge his confession, and that is somehow worse than if she had. It suggests her expectations of him are right where he has always feared they would one day end up, and where they themselves are now: somewhere south of nowhere.

"Let's not let Cody hear that, all right? I don't want to scare him."

He nods his agreement. "I don't think we have anything to worry about there. If anything he seems to be *enjoying* this."

"Well, you promised an adventure. Looks like he's having one."

It was supposed to be an adventure for them all. A more stable, more carefree couple might still have been able to view it as one. But stable they are not, and labeling this an adventure now would only be a form of denial.

"I still can't believe it's even possible to get lost in this day and age," she says.

"People get lost all the time."

"I know, but..." She gestures helplessly at the dark theater of their surroundings, her flashlight illuminating the sinuously moving boughs above their heads. "We didn't camp that far from the trail, did we? I mean, shouldn't it have been easier to find? How did we go so far off track?"

There is no accusation in her tone, but his conscience is a lot less forgiving. He had, in actual fact, disregarded the suggestion (warning) from the camp attendant in favor of a more out of the way (prohibited) area, a more great outdoorsy (unincorporated) place rather than the large, fenced-in patch of worn earth they would have had to share with two other couples (both of whom had had much more impressive tents and so were probably safe and dry right now). In his youth he'd gone camping with his father a few times, and those occasions were some of the best moments of his life. He had hoped in keeping with the wildness of the location, he could recreate the spirit of those cherished trips, could reproduce with his own family the bond he'd forged with his father. Back then you didn't need to book a place, or get anybody's permission. You just geared up and went hiking until you found the perfect spot to set up stakes. The real, honest-to-goodness camping experience. And if something went wrong, well, that was part of the adventure too.

But now, in place of adventure, there was only misery and panic that increased exponentially with every mile they covered.

"After the tent blew away," he admits, "I thought I was leading us back to the trail. I guess I got turned around."

"Should we try to find a shelter, maybe under one of the bigger trees? Maybe light a fire or something? We'll freeze out here."

"We're under the only kind of shelter this part of the woods offers and we're still getting soaked. Best to just keep moving for now, like you said. I'm sure we'll come across a ranger station or something sooner or later."

"A ranger station? We're in Hocking Hills, Mike, not Yellowstone. How much research did you do before you dragged us up here? You're more likely to find a moonshine still here than a ranger station."

"Hell, right now I'd settle for that." When she doesn't return his smile, he continues, "But seriously, there are a few cabins around these woods. We saw one of them on the way up here, remember? We're sure to come across one if we soldier on a bit further."

"Cabins, sure," she says, and gives a slight shake of her head, "Which begs the question why you didn't just book one of *those* instead of insisting we rough it."

And there it is. This time there was no attempt to keep the resentment from her tone. Gone is the levity, the ceasefire, the pretense that anything is going to be all right. Juliet slamming the window shut on poor old Romeo. And now he knows they have to keep moving, have to find a way out of this damn weather and this predicament, because with every hour that passes in these godforsaken woods, they are getting more and more lost, the rift he had hoped to heal widening with every step they take in the wrong direction. The storm is softening the walls of his marital house, the rain implanting mold beneath the plaster, and soon it will weaken them, force them to crumble until the whole place comes crashing down.

"Sorry," he mutters too low for her to hear over the wind that makes the trees sound as if their branches are laden with snakes. He turns and manages half a step before Emma's hand slams down on his shoulder, startling a cry from him, her nails digging into his flesh through the thin protection of his slicker. Hissing pain through his teeth, he turns and sees her face has turned white, whiter than before. She has become a ghost with coals for eyes, and fear colder than the wind, colder than the rain seizes him, just as it appears to have seized her.

"Emma, what—?"

"*Cody*," she all but screams at him, the rain streaming down her face making her look as if she's melting before him.

His confusion evaporates as he looks over her shoulder.

The boy is gone.

* * *

"He can't have gone far," he tells her, struggling to keep the panic from his voice.

"Really?" She has fallen into step behind him, one hand clutched on his backpack to steady herself as she makes her treacherous way across the deadfall. It has the effect of adding her weight to his already cumbersome load. "So finally you've gotten a handle on direction, have you?"

"God damn it, leave me alone," he mutters under his breath, then curses when his foot comes down on a patch of ground that's not ground at all, but a water-filled hollow. Cold water seeps into his boot up to the laces. The burst blister on his heel catches fire.

Lightning flares, turning the tree trunks to stone and sending thick spears of shadow into the cobalt spaces between them, but they reveal nothing to Mike but more felled trees, scrub, and waterlogged forest floor.

As they march back the way they came, pausing every few seconds in the lulls between flares of lightning to lance with their flashlight beams the boil of the steaming dark, Mike knows it's time to give up, not on the boy, no, never that, but himself. All that matters now is finding Cody and getting them all out of here. And once he does—

what then? Divorce, probably. He's tired, just as worn out as Emma, and just as sick of trying so hard for little reward. He may be naïve in certain ways, but he's far from stupid. And a man would have to be some kind of dumb not to be able to read the signals his wife has been sending him for the past eight months. She's done, and if he had any sense at all, he'd be done too. All this trying to make her change her mind about him, about *them*, has done nothing but make him appear sad and desperate, which he is, and it's exhausting, and it makes him hate himself.

Sometimes, it even makes him angry, though he's never quite sure at whom that anger is directed.

Right now, she's making it a little easier to for him to focus that anger.

He stops to wait as she clamps her flashlight between her knees, raises her hands to cup her mouth, and cries out the boy's name. He has already told her Cody won't hear her over the storm, but she's a mother, and mothers don't listen to anything but their own hearts when it comes to their children.

As he sweeps his light across the boles, fear twists his guts. They will find the boy—he knows this, has to believe they will—but this interim, the waiting until they do, is terrifying. Their attention was only away from the boy for a few minutes, so he truly believed what he had told Emma: The boy could not have gone far. Probably just snuck behind a tree to take a whizz, in which case moving further away from where they'd been was probably an even worse idea.

"Emma," he says, when she pauses to take a breath to power another cry for the boy.

She looks at him, eyes dark with anger, electric with fear. "What?"

"We shouldn't go any further."

"We have to find him. We have to find where he is."

"I know." A wild gust of wind strong enough to make him stagger drowns out his words, and he waits for it to abate. *We're doing everything wrong.* Pulling his hood tight against his face to protect himself from the needling of the icy rain, he tries again. "I know, but I figure he just went to find some privacy so he could take a leak, maybe." *Please let that be it.*

Hope reduces some of the darkness in her eyes as the idea takes hold. "So what do we do?"

"We go back to where we were and wait there. If he comes back and we're not where he left us, we'll lose him for sure."

She nods. "Okay, but let's hurry."

He does, and together they retrace their steps for a second time. At least this time, they know where they're going. Along the way, in a stroke of luck Mike is almost afraid to acknowledge lest it reverse itself out of spite, the rain begins to ease off, the wind to lessen to a bluster, like a belligerent drunk losing steam. And by the time they reach the spot where they last saw Cody, the area memorable only because of a half-buried sandstone boulder protruding from the mud and deadfall like the shoulder-bone of a felled giant, the rain stops completely. Mike yanks down his hood and takes a deep breath, as if they have spent the past few hours not in a storm, but underwater, and leans back against the boulder, grateful for the temporary reprieve from the backpack's weight.

"So, where the hell is he?" Emma asks, and when he looks at her, he sees the anger has returned. He watches her pallor deepen as the storm clouds scatter, uncovering a three-quarter moon that somehow looks as stained and wretched as the boulder upon which he rests. Unzipping his windbreaker and shrugging off the pack, he raises a hand. "Just a second."

Her body thrums with impatience. "You're just going to sit there?"

"My feet hurt. Trust me, he'll be here. We just need to wait."

She stares at him for a moment. It only takes another one for her to be in his face.

And at last, the dam breaks.

"Wait? Trust you? Neither of those suggestions sound reasonable to me, Mike. We've been waiting for hours for you to show some sign that you're even slightly capable of getting us out of this mess, despite there being no evidence of you being able to do anything of the kind as long as we've known you."

We. Mike wonders if perhaps his earlier paranoia about what she might be saying to the boy was not so misguided, after all.

Her voice is very loud in the eerie stillness left in the wake of the storm.

"And: trust you? That's all I've ever done, Mike, is trust you, and look where it's gotten me. I gave up my job because you promised to take care of me, even though I loved being a teacher. You said 'trust you' then too. I look forward to the vacations you promise you'll get us with your bonus every year but those vacations never happen because the fucking *bonuses* never happen. And I'm still waiting for you to take care of *me*. But instead what I get is you forever looking at me waiting for me to tell you everything's all right, that I'm happy with you, that nothing's your fault. All you want are reassurances that I still love you, that I'm happy with you, when you've never been able to provide good enough reasons for that to still be the case. You moon about looking as if you believe nobody *should* love you. And maybe you're right."

The color has returned to her face, the fury warming her from the inside out. Her breath steams in her face as she rages; her eyes glitter like elliptical shards of volcanic rock. "So here I am, a prisoner of my own cowardice, trapped in a marriage of habit, forty-seven years of age with my looks gone to shit, my weight all over the place, and I'm stuck in these goddamn woods with *you*. My son is missing, none of us even wanted to *be* here. I fucking *hate* the woods, Mike. I don't know how many times I've told you that, but because *you* like them, here we are, and now that it's gone to shit like everything else you touch, you've been looking at me with your sad eyes for hours hoping I'll take pity on you and as usual tell you it isn't your fault. Well, you want to know something, Mike? It damn well *is* your fault. *Every* time you fuck up, it's your fault, because you're a gutless piece of shit who makes life miserable for everyone because that's all you know how to do. You waste away at a job you despise, transferring calls to everyone else because—and I swear this should be your motto—"It's Not Your Department". And I hate it, Mike. I fucking *hate* the way you suck the life from me. I hate the way you mope around depending on me, and on Cody, to make you feel better about yourself, and to make for you your excuses for the way you are, and I hate…I…" Breathing hard, she shakes her head and brings her hands up to cover her face. Then she turns away from him, her body convulsing as she begins to sob.

Mike sits stunned, the wind knocked from his sails as he tries to digest what she has just said. It is as if the storm passed because she inhaled it, only to vomit it forth again into his face. Never in all their years together has he seen her lose her temper like this, at least not with him. He has seen her frustrated, irritated, morose. He has never seen her become the storm, and it leaves him confused. He opens his mouth to apologize until he realizes that's all he ever does. So instead he waits, takes a deep breath, and in time, allows some of the storm to infect him too, allows his own anger to leak into his throat, an emotion forced into being by the absolute absence of all others in the face of her attack.

"Finish what you were saying."

Still with her back to him, she asks, "What?"

"You were listing the things you hate. There was something else on that list. What was it? Was it me? Were you going to say that you hate me?"

She steps closer to the rank of poplars and beech and calls out for their son, her distress causing her voice to crack on the second syllable. Without the storm for competition, her voice carries far and clear, echoing through the trees long after she has fallen quiet. If Cody is anywhere close by at all, he will hear her.

"Were you going to say you hate me?" Mike repeats, and pushes away from the boulder. The backpack slides off the rock and crumples to the soft earth. He leaves it there and takes a step closer to his wife. A timid voice inside him, the same one that has kept him quiet, kept him characterized as weak his whole life, advises he stay silent until the smoke has cleared from this particular blaze. But he doesn't want to, not now, maybe not ever again. Incredibly, for a man unaccustomed to giving up on anyone but himself, he thinks he may have found the real reason for this seemingly ill-advised jaunt into the woods. He thinks he might have brought Emma here to find out, not if she still loves him or if there is anything left to save, but to find out if *he* still loves *her,* if he *wants* there to be something left to save. Because right at this moment, he is emboldened and reinvigorated to find that he might not, and that he might finally have the words to tell her as much.

The canopy drips fat, cold drops of rainwater down upon them. Steam from hot earth cooled by the storm rises in a lazy mist around their legs. Emma screams for Cody again, keeps her back to her husband, her shoulders tensing through her slicker at the sound of his approach. She folds her arms tightly. *Of course she does,* thinks Mike, *in keeping with frigid tradition.*

"Were you?" he asks again, drawing to a halt a few feet behind her.

"Just…just stop, Mike. Please," she says. "I shouldn't have said anything. Let's just focus on what's important. I just want to find

Cody and get out of here."

As she cups her mouth again, preparing another summons for their wayward son, he grabs her by the shoulders, perhaps not hard enough to hurt, but harder than she is used to, at least. The surprise on her face is a wonderful thing. He relishes it, thinks that maybe he could get used to having her look at him that way again, because he's pretty sure the last time she looked at him with any respect, was on the day he first opened the door to her all those many years ago. But of course, she didn't know him then.

Sir, are you a registered voter in the state of Ohio? Good, then if I might have a couple of minutes of your time...?

He'd been willing to give her the rest of his life. But now, rather abruptly and terrifyingly, he is no longer sure that's still the case. Because he was not altogether surprised to hear that she has accumulated her share of misgivings over the course of their marriage, even if hearing them hurt. Such things stand to reason. But she might be surprised to learn that he has misgivings of his own, chief among them one she threw back in his own face: trust, or more specifically, the lack of it.

"Where was all of this during counseling?" he asks. "Counseling that *you* suggested and *I* paid for. Where was all of this when it might have done some good, huh?"

She will not meet his gaze.

"If you hate me, I've probably earned it," he tells her, even as she jerks free of his grip and glares at him. "But you've never had cause to question my loyalty. Answer me that, at least: have you?"

"I'm not doing this right now," she says, and turns away from him again. It punches a hot steel rod of anger through his belly and he has to struggle to resist the urge to grab her and *force* her back around to look at him. But he knows that'll bring him dangerously close to a dark, forbidden place, one from which he will never be able to return.

"You had no problem giving me a rundown of my failures, babe," he says. "So you can at least admit to one of yours."

"I don't know what you're talking about."

That small voice again, pleading for reason: *Don't say it. Don't open this door. Not here, not now.*

He ignores it, taking no small measure of glee in not merely opening but kicking off the hinges a door which has long been locked to him, the contents of the room beyond a maddening mystery.

"Wednesday nights. Where do you go?"

And now she does turn to face him, whips down her own hood, her features twisted into a look of confusion. "What?"

"You heard me."

"Are you seriously asking me this? Now?"

"Yes. Where do you go on Wednesday nights? It's a simple question."

"I go to the book club. You know that."

"What book club?"

"What book...? You're losing it, Mike. Big time. And I'm not playing this game, whatever it is."

"Yes you are."

Her eyes flash anger again, and this time despite the confidence lent him by his own resentment and certainty of betrayal, it gives him pause, tells him that perhaps his suspicions are indeed wrong. Even if they're not, he is not sure he will ever be able to get her to admit that to him. Her constitution has always been the stronger one.

"Let me ask you where *you* think I go, Mike, since you're the one who doubts me."

Last chance, Mike. Last chance to keep your mouth shut and spare yourself the last shovel of grave dirt.

But the words are too far up his throat, too tantalizing on his tongue for him to swallow them now. "That book club stopped meeting at the library eight weeks ago. I checked."

She hesitates, then starts to answer, and he knows by the ugly mask her face has become that he is not going to like whatever she has to say, but then her head whips around and she gasps, backs away from him, her arm extending to point at the rank of trees, or something between them. "Mike."

His anger had not been easy to generate. His whole life he has avoided confrontation because he has never been adept at it. It did in fact require his wife's near-admission of her hatred of him for him to even know he was capable of such ire, and even then it came from fear of rejection, of abandonment, of being forced to be alone yet again. But he finds now that it drains quickly in the face of whatever it is she may have seen. And with the reminder of where they are and what they are doing, shame burns his cheeks. *Jesus Christ, Mike*, he thinks. *Your son...*

"What is it?" he asks, and steps close, follows her gaze.

"There," she tells him, pointing at something between the trees, her own anger gone, replaced by fragile hope. "Do you see it?"

For a moment he doesn't, and feels his heart sinking, but then…there it is, a soft amber glow winking at them through the phalanx of trees from somewhere in the distance. It calls to mind the light of a ship or a buoy on a dark sea.

"Is it him?" Emma asks, though of course there is no way to know.

"Let's find out," he says, and offers her his hand. She looks at it for a moment, then brings her gaze to meet his, both of their faces chalk-white in the moonlight. There is no apology in her eyes, but no anger either, only the acceptance, however temporary, of a truce for the greater good. Then she takes his hand, her skin cold, and they aim their flashlights ahead of them and plunge into the woods.

* * *

In the thick of the trees, the ground begins to rise again, which is not good. It tells Mike they are moving even further off track (wherever the hell the track *is*), ascending the moon-shadow hill instead of descending to the valley where the chance of finding the campground is greater. But that's all right for now, because there is a light, the first one they've seen since losing their way. Best case scenario, it *is* Cody, demonstrating better sense than his parents did and waiting instead of roaming aimlessly through the enormous woods in search of them. If it's not, then Mike knows his heart is going to shatter and Emma will be inconsolable, but it might be a cabin, and from there they might be able to summon help and end this nightmare. And though he does not want to think about rescue choppers and search teams, and the horrifying possibility of never finding their son (especially considering what he and Emma will forever remember doing when they should have been looking for him), he wants even less to wander these woods indefinitely waiting to freeze or starve to death. His wife's words come back to him: *I still can't believe it's even possible to get lost in this day and age.* And while of course such a thing is possible—it happens all the time—he didn't think it possible *here*, not in a stretch of woods less than an hour from their home. Abroad, maybe, where everything would seem alien, but not here, not somewhere he could probably see the Columbus skyline if he climbed high enough.

But all he has seen for the past three hours, and all he fears he will ever see again, are more and more trees.

"You all right?" he asks his wife, and she looks at him, her face barely lit by the glow from her flashlight.

"No," she replies.

They're cold and miserable and out of their depth, the tension between them far from eradicated, only on hold for the time being. The argument both incensed and demoralized him, like ice water thrown on a burning man, leaving him numb, and now he finds himself investing everything he has left in that little light. It might be a lantern, his son's or a hunter's flashlight, a candle in the window of a welcoming home or a manned outpost…it is not yet possible to tell. But what it represents is a promise of sanctuary, however temporary, and so they skid and strain their way against the rocky, slippery slope, heartened by its unwavering glow.

It takes them the better part of forty minutes before the slope levels out and they find themselves in a clearing. There they stop, exhausted. Mike doubles over, hands on his knees, his heart hammering so hard it must surely be digging its way out of his chest, while Emma surveys the area.

"Cory?" she says, her voice low, as if afraid of disturbing someone.

Ringed by gnarled and ancient oak trees, the clearing is roughly forty, no more than fifty feet in diameter, the floor carpeted with the same woodland detritus they've been battling their way through all night: twisted scrub, broken branches, twigs, and dead leaves, though here and there are bare patches of earth and what appear to be a scattering of small dark boulders. It is an unremarkable place, otherwise disappointing to Mike but for the tent that squats upon one of those patches. Once he has caught his breath, he straightens, knees, back, and feet aching, but does not move. Emma stands a few feet away from him, staring at the tent and similarly immobile, and though she doesn't say a word, he knows what has given her pause, can see it just as clearly as she can.

The tent is unlike any he has ever seen before, and yet somehow it reminds him of his own. Perhaps it is the dark yellow hue, or the dome-like shape, but there the similarities to his ill-advised purchase end. The longer he looks at it, the better it makes him feel about his own dubious skill as an outdoorsman, because clearly whoever erected this tent didn't even know that the tent poles or rods or whatever the heck they're called, usually go on the inside. Then again, the rods themselves don't look like the traditional kind either. Dark brown, ropy and knuckled, and curving down from an arched and similarly knuckled spine-like ridge along the top of the tent, they appear to be made from flexible sticks or branches, so Mike wonders if perhaps, rather than looking at the work of an amateur, he's observing the work of a *true* frontiersman, someone who perhaps, in losing their own tent in the inclement weather, had the resourcefulness to fashion a crude one from the materials at hand. The roof and sides of the tent appear to have been fashioned using vellum, or similar material, thin enough to allow the small orb of light within to be seen from without. There are no pegs or guy lines, and odder still, no entrance that he can see, though it's possible they're looking at the back of it.

Emma turns to look at him. "Do you think he might be in there?"

He doesn't, because the soft amber light inside the tent is unobstructed and casts no shadows against its walls, but he takes a moment to weigh up the wisdom of sharing this opinion. He settles for a noncommittal "Not sure," and takes a few steps further into the clearing and looks around even though there is little to be seen. "But if nothing else, it could be a place to stop and regroup." As soon as he uses the word, he regrets it, because the terrible truth is that their *group* is one short, and he knows that they were counting on finding Cody behind that light, beckoning them toward him with his flashlight. More than once, Mike even imagined he saw the boy's fuzzy silhouette waiting for them in the darkness behind that glow. But now they're here, and Cody isn't, and the implications of that fact are enough to suck the life from him, to hammer ingots of despair and hopelessness into his brain.

Please God, let him be all right. Whatever the price I need to pay, I'll gladly pay it. Just please, please, let my boy be okay.

But he refuses to give up, at least not yet. He has to hold it together for Emma's sake, for Cody's sake. Whatever happens, they need to stay alert and vigilant, need to focus on reclaiming their son from the cold, dark woods. Because if anything has happened to their boy, it will alter for them both the definition of lost. There will, quite simply, be no more reason for them to go on. They may have their differences, may even have to go their separate ways and concede defeat when all of this is over, but the boy is an innocent and should not be made to pay for his unflagging faith in his guardians, in the people sworn to protect him. If such faith ends up costing the boy his life, then Mike and Emma will be guilty of the ultimate failure, and it will kill them, and the punishment will fit the crime.

He turns his head and looks at the tent. "It didn't just pop up out of the ground," he mumbles.

Emma draws closer to him, her fingers finding the crook of his arm in a tenderness borne of anxiety, not love, from the accurate assumption that he has become just as fragile as she has. "What?"

"The tent. It'd be one thing if we just stumbled upon somebody's old abandoned camping ground, but the tent's in pretty good shape from what I can see, and there's a light on, which means somebody used it, and recently. And people don't just walk off and leave their stuff behind, right?" *Unless they're people like us,* he thinks miserably, picturing the backpack he left by the boulder somewhere down there at the foot of the hill, and the tent they abandoned, though technically the tent abandoned *them.* "So there's a good chance whoever owns this thing will come back, and they can help us."

Encouraged, Emma nods. "Okay, that makes sense."

In the distance, thunder rumbles. A light rain starts to fall, pattering like insistent fingers on their slickers.

"Shit," Mike says, feeling his spirits fall in time with the silvery threads. "Looks like the dry spell is over."

"Should we wait inside it?" Emma asks, training her flashlight beam at the side of the tent and bleaching out the interior amber glow. "I mean, you don't think whoever owns it would mind, do you? Considering the circumstances? At least we'd be out of the rain."

For a moment, Mike doesn't answer, because he doesn't know what to say other than that he doesn't think that's a good idea at all. Considering all that's gone wrong this night, the strange little tent is a godsend. And yet, for no reason he can express in words, the more he looks at it, the more he realizes that he would rather continue to brave the storm than crawl inside it. It's a preposterous thing to feel, and he knows this, and yet the potency of his sudden, inexplicable aversion to the tent seems justification enough.

You're being ridiculous.

This he knows, but still…

"I'm not sure that's the best idea," he says.

"For Heaven's sake, why?"

"I don't know, just a feeling. We don't know who owns it, or how they might react to finding us inside. Could be a hunter's camp."

"So?"

"The kind of hunter who might mistake us for scavengers and shoot before asking questions."

"Like it or not, we *are* scavengers now, Mike. And if there's food in there, I don't mind telling you, I'm going to help myself. Coffee, the same."

He has to admit the idea of sustenance sounds tempting. They haven't eaten anything since stopping at a Wendy's on their way to the hills. When was that? Five, six hours ago? His mouth waters, his body prematurely warming to the thought of hot coffee gushing down his throat, melting the ice inside him and chasing away some of the dread.

And yet it is that same dread that holds him in place as he studies the yellow object with the odd branch-like trim. He notices it doesn't move, seems resistant to the wind.

Which is perhaps what a good, expensive, reliable tent does, *Mike, not that you'd know anything about it. Yours was a discount item because you were more concerned with your bank balance than the safety of your family. It's a* tent, *for God's sake, nothing more, and all you're doing now is all you've ever done: making dubious choices and stalling when affirmative action would yield a more sensible result,* chides the voice of reason, a voice that might have made Mike's life a whole lot better if he had acknowledged its counsel even once over the years. But instinct will not allow him to heed it now.

"Let's just wait a while, okay? Out here."

He knows she's going to argue, and doesn't blame her. The woods are getting to him. The cold and the rain and the hunger and the desperation have combined to make a scrambled mess of his brains. The enormity of what has happened to them, of what his misguided need to bond with his family has caused to happen is debilitating. The thought of waiting here while Cody wanders the woods alone and frightened is enough to make him want to tear his own heart out, but he doesn't know what else to do. His wife, like his own inner voice, will argue that he's circumventing wisdom, as always, making the situation more difficult than it already is. And she'll be right, and he will have no comeback. Because the only thing he can think to say will only make him appear insane, and even more pathetic than his actions thus far have allowed: *I'm afraid of it, Emma. The tent. I can't explain why, so please don't ask me. It just feels wrong, feels like someone drew us here on purpose. One light in the whole damn woods, in a part of the woods nobody's supposed to go, and it leads us here, to a tent with nobody in it. It just feels* wrong.

"Out here?" Emma says. "So we can get soaked all over again. What's the matter with you?"

To give him time to compose a reply good enough to placate her—assuming such a reply exists—he carefully makes his way to the nearest one of the small boulders. He needs to sit down, to take the weight off his feet, because it feels as if the backs of his hiking boots have eaten their way clean through to the bone. But as he nears the boulder, he sees that it is not a boulder at all, but some kind of shrub. Closer still and his light reveals that it is more like tumbleweed, though more densely constructed and much bigger than any he has ever seen. It reaches almost to his waist.

"Emma, come take a look at this," he says, raising his light to shoulder height and aiming the beam downward like a mechanic inspecting the guts of a troublesome vehicle.

"What now?"

Despite the cold sensation of dread that crawls like the rain down the back of his neck, Mike is fascinated at his discovery.

The object before him is a rough oval composite of grass, sticks, and coarse thin fibers he identifies as animal hair, and as he runs a tentative hand over the top of the tightly woven mass, the twigs like hard, slick tendrils in the rain, he is once again transported via memory back to his youth, this time to Mrs. Edgerton's biology class on the day when she got them all to study owl pellets. He recalls being repulsed as he pulled apart the small, hairy brown orb of compacted waste matter, only to find his sense of wonder inflamed at the sight of what was revealed to him: several smooth tiny stones, desiccated insect remains, and the skeleton of a mouse. *Indigestible material,* Mrs. Edgerton had informed the class with her trademark haughty, holier-than-thou delivery, *which in its excretion also helps cleanse the gullet of the animal.*

Mike shakes his head. What he is looking at couldn't possibly be the same manner of thing, could it? *Not unless they have birds the size of my Toyota up here.* Deferring to that sense of childhood wonder again, he pins the flashlight under his chin, the light angled toward the top of the tumbleweed-thing, and braces his knees against the object for support—thereby discovering that it is heavy enough to resist being moved by his weight—and, carefully slipping his fingers into the latticework of branches of which the outer shell is composed, pulls the thing apart. It opens easily, the top portion splitting wide with the sound of firecrackers, and Mike stumbles back a step as a noxious smell of methane rises in an invisible cloud to envelop him. Coughing, he waves a hand before his face, eyes wide with incredulity, and, the flashlight trembling in his hand from the cocktail of cold, fatigue, and terror, leans over to inspect his handiwork.

"Honey…" he says, his voice very small. "You're not going to believe this…"

His efforts have not sundered the object enough for him to see straight down into its center. He has only managed to yank open an upper section of its bulk, but it's enough. On the tightly woven bed of straw, wiry animal hair, and undigested plant matter he has exposed, the light shows a large portion of bone, and perhaps it is only because he has already summoned the memory of his high school biology class that he understands that the bone, scratched and striated and shiny in the rain, does not belong to an animal.

But the red collar with the little silver bell most certainly does.

He straightens, moves away from the giant pellet-thing and slowly sweeps his juddering flashlight beam to his left, to the three other "boulders" he registered on the way in, then to his right, where there are two more, laying on their sides like giant, dark Easter eggs. From one of them pokes what he earlier took to be the dead branch of a silver birch and now acknowledges is more likely the leg-bone of an animal, probably a deer. A cold current floods his body. And in his shock, the only thing that runs through his mind is a simple, logical fact, a ridiculously obvious observation that nonetheless terrifies him to his core.

Waste follows feeding.

He takes another step backward, his throat clenching against the magnificently irresistible need to scream until his lungs burst, because now he knows something else. Cavemen did not need prior knowledge or textbooks or common sense to know when they were being hunted. They felt it on an instinctual, primal level. And that, he concludes, even as his composure threatens to collapse like a shoddily built wall, is what *he* felt as soon as they stepped foot into the clearing.

"Hello?" he hears his wife ask, and knows it is not directed at him. The sound of that word paints a picture of what he's going to see when he turns around and his body goes rigid. Because even though what he has just found is not sufficient evidence to identify the tent as the source of the danger he feels crawling all over him now like an army of fire ants, instinct tells him it is, and it is on this instinct he realizes he should have relied.

"Emma," he says. "Don't."

"I found the opening," she replies.

His paralysis breaks and he turns, his flashlight sweeping an arc of luminescence through the rain. "Emma, no!"

She is down on her haunches, pulling back a large leathery flap at the far end of the tent, the end that was hidden from them when they entered the clearing. The look on her face as she does so does nothing to assuage his dread. It is a look of repulsion, one he has come to know very well for all the wrong reasons during the course of his marriage to this woman, and when she releases the flap, it remains connected to her fingers by long thick translucent strands of mucous. And although he feels himself running to her, reaching out to grab her and yank her away from there, he can't move. In what is perhaps a sign of impending insanity, the voice inside his head becomes that of the marriage counselor, that enviably handsome Doctor White, with the perfect teeth and expensive clothes, who probably never had problems with a woman, or a man, for that matter, in his whole damn life, saying words he never would have said out loud:

You've wanted to run for years, haven't you Mike. You've just never had the courage.

No, that isn't—

And now you can. Because this situation doesn't require courage. Just the opposite. All you need to do here is give in to your instinctual need for self-preservation, and run. Problem solved.

No. I won't. I can't.

Sure you can. Because as much an outsider as you may have always felt, you're out of your element for real right here. This isn't your world. People are forbidden from coming here for a very good reason. And right now, you're looking at it.

This, Mikey, is most definitely Not Your Department.

Mike drops the flashlight and, screaming his wife's name, runs toward the tent, his heels and shins raging with pain, the panic in his throat threatening to strangle him. And as he closes the distance, he sees Emma, the woman he knows he loves despite her doubts, the counselor's doubts, and even his own, look up at him in confusion, her hands still held out before her in disgust, the glistening mess dripping from between her fingers. In an instant, at the sight of him, his primal terror is transferred to her eyes. Swallowing, unwilling to wait to find out why her husband is hobbling toward her in insane panic, she starts to stand.

"Mike, what—?"

The back end of the tent deflates as if crushed under the foot of an invisible giant. At the same time, the ridged spine, so like a thorny branch, arches itself and the flaps at the front snap open like batwings, partially obscuring what happens next.

Emma screams; Mike stumbles over a knotted mess of branches and goes down, badly scraping his hands and knees, and the tent begins to shudder.

Up on his tortured feet again and he's alongside the thing, almost within grabbing distance of his wife, close enough now to see that the soft light inside the tent-that-is-not-a-tent is glowing like a sun, close enough to see the network of thin, dark blue veins threading like worms through its vellum-like skin, close enough to hear his wife draw in a breath to scream.

But the scream never comes. Like a javelin thrown with great force from inside the tent, a long wormy, segmented appendage with an end that tapers to a wickedly sharp point of bone explodes from inside the thing and punctures his wife's throat just below her larynx. She jolts, her eyes opening wide as moons that stare upward at nothing. She convulses, feet kicking at the ground and releases the breath in a gurgle that forces red bubbles out around the spike of bone that has penetrated her. The appendage shudders as if in desire as Emma's body sags, the life draining away even as her mucous-slimed hands beat weakly at the thing that has invaded her, but her protests are feeble and short-lived.

For a moment, it seems to Mike as if the world has been paused. Even the rain seems to slow. He drops to his knees, knowing he could still reach out and grab Emma's hand, knowing too that it's too late. In a panic, he sleeves tears away from his eyes, fearing they will blind him to some supernatural reversal of this horrific moment, or to some opportunity to undo it, and sees only the retraction of that appendage, withdrawn as quickly as it came, pulling his wife off her knees as if she were a rag doll. And then she is gone, with a small pool of blood the only sign that she was there at all, and the rain works hard to erase even that. The tent begins to undulate, the light within flickering and throwing the shadow of his wife against its skin as it feeds on her. His wife, and a hint of what murdered her.

At the sight of it, he feels or imagines he feels a small pop as the bubble of his sanity breaks, and an involuntary sob escapes him.

As if in response, the undulation of the tent halts.

Listening.

Mike claps his hands over his mouth, one over the other, madness and stark, raving terror pulsing between his eyes.

He cannot move, cannot breathe, doesn't dare. All he can do is watch, as, after a prolonged moment, the creature resumes its feeding. And as the rain grows heavier, each drop that taps against his head brings with it words he has learned in the years since Mrs. Edgerton's biology class. Words like: *bioluminescence, lure, camouflage, adaptation, imitation,* and perhaps just as accurate: *stingray, scorpion, crawfish, bat, arachnid.* None of these attributes or comparisons seems outlandish to him now, for in the shadow theater the interior of the tent-that-is-not-a-tent has become, he sees the impression of something that is all of these things and none of them. The large black mass at the epicenter calls to mind a fat black spider in its web, legs working busily as it rends his wife's body asunder, the bulk of its body extending down from the ridged spine. Spindly, knuckled arms connect bat-like to the sides (wings?) of the tent. Looking at it in its real form, Mike wonders how anyone could have mistaken it for something benign, but then, isn't that the point of camouflage? How many others, he wonders, as he slowly, ever-so-slowly rises to his feet, have gotten lost in the storm and been lured to their deaths at this creature's hands/claws/wings by the promise of shelter?

The answer, he supposes, lie in the tumbleweed-like mounds around him.

And it is to one of these mounds that he moves, limping around the puddles, careful to make as little noise as possible. Facing the tent-thing, but averting his eyes as his wife's blood splashes the inside of its membranous walls and the thing shudders in ecstasy, he tries to keep the shock from turning him to stone.

It's okay to run now, Mr. Sellers, says the counselor.

"No, it isn't," Mike whispers. "It never was. And the first thing I'm going to do when, and if, I get back to Columbus, is punch your perfect fucking teeth in."

The counselor is quiet, and Mike finds solace in his anger, finds that it is all he has left. As he inches away from the tent toward the mound nearest the point where he and Emma entered the clearing, he tries not to think of Cody, because whenever he does, he sees him not as he was in life, but as a collection of stained and scratched undigested bones nestled in a clotted ovum of this creature's waste. As likely a fate as that might be, Mike refuses to believe it until confirmation presents itself, assuming it ever does. If there is a modicum of relief to be found in the chaotic nightmare his world has become, it is that the bone he saw inside that mound was adult-sized.

Cody then, might yet be alive, and this alone is reason enough to even consider resistance in the face of such an impossible aberration.

When he bumps up against one of the mounds, he stops, and reluctantly casts a glance at the tent. Blinks his eyes clear of the worsening rain. Whatever is left of his wife is not anything resembling a human now. The silhouette of the spider/crawfish/bat-thing is poking with spindly legs at a ragged, shapeless shadow it holds in its clutches, as if testing its tenderness.

Mike, trembling uncontrollably, and wishing the calm he felt were a good thing instead of an obvious sign that he has jumped headlong into the abyss he has feared as long as he's been on the earth, drops his gaze to the sodden ground between his feet, and the long leg-bone he spotted earlier. This close, it looks smaller and thinner, but given the circumstances, he figures it will be better than harsh words as a weapon. He drops down and tugs the bone free from the tangled latticework of the creature's waste, wonders as he rises if he has time to try and break it, to make it sharper, wonders if there's any point. And then he realizes it is not a bone at all, but a lovingly carved walking stick with a knuckled top. Remembers his own grandfather having a similar one, though perhaps it was a little less intricate and well-cared for as this one. Remembers because the old man used to hit him across the back with it when he was drunk. *You're just as worthless as your father, you little shit.* And the memory angers him.

And what do you plan to do with that? the counselor pipes up, sounding sulky from his earlier chastisement. *What do you think it will let you do with it? It'll snatch it away from you and use it to pick pieces of you and your poor wife from between its teeth.*

"Sh-shut up," Mike says, through chattering teeth.

Why not just throw stones at it instead?

Mike begins to limp his way back toward the tent, his body numb but his senses honed to the same sharp point absent from his weapon, as they must be when facing death. Emma is dead, Cody is missing, and no matter what hope he might try to siphon from the situation, on the only level resistant to denial, he knows everything is lost. His world, which he has fooled himself into thinking has always been some broad, endless thing, has been reduced to this clearing, and the thing that lives here, the hostile creature that has removed from him all that ever mattered. And though he is aware that the chances of inflicting damage on the creature are practically nonexistent—he imagines that appendage shooting out and killing him before he even has a chance to draw back the walking stick—there is quite simply nothing left to do. If he runs, if he was able enough to run, it would be on him in an instant. And even if it turns out that the malevolent thing is confined to this clearing and as such cannot give chase—so what? What kind of life awaits him now outside of this killing ground, beyond the place where everything was taken from him in a few short hours? No, he led his family into this horror, into this slaughter, and without them, there is no reason to leave.

Because instinct tells him his son is dead. He has not explored the other mounds, nor will he. The odds of his son's survival, already significantly reduced when they lost him, are, in the face of the unexpected horror these woods have been hiding, now practically nonexistent.

So here it must end, with a being he would never have dared believe existed outside of mad fantasy, a creature that if he were forced to describe to any rational person would no doubt elicit laughter and doubts about his sanity. They would label him a murderer because it would be the logical verdict. *No, Officer, it wasn't me, it was a tent!* He snorts involuntary laughter and then raises his free hand to stifle it. But it's difficult because indeed his enemy, the true murderer, *is* a laughable, incredible thing. But quickly the humor ebbs away, replaced by that welcome numbness as he brings his gaze to bear on the monster before him.

In the flesh, what he's looking at is not funny in the least. It is the stuff of nightmare, of the horror shows his mother kept on mute. And how he wishes he could mute all of this now, just shut out the world and wait for the broadcast to end and his life to go off the air.

Not for your ears, Mikey.

And not for his eyes.

Five feet from the tent, the light inside it goes out, and the creature is still.

Mike stops too, his breath coming in harsh rasps that send clouds of vapor steaming into the air, heating his cheeks only briefly. The rain continues to sizzle down around him. Uncertainty keeps him immobile, and faced with the abruptly dormant antagonist, a feeble red pulse of panic flares deep within him.

I could run. He envisions himself dropping the walking stick—and he admits now that he is in complete if reluctant agreement with the counselor regarding its efficacy as a weapon—and quietly making his way out of the clearing, imagines the darkness between the trees appearing to go on forever, walking for miles in the rain, defeated, drained by grief. And then a light, a break in the trees, another clearing, only this time the light that finds him is not the insidious lure of some unknowable predator, but the real light of a log cabin, its chimney trailing smoke he can smell from where he stands, dumbfounded. He sees the cabin door opening, revealing the firelight within, and a man standing in the doorway, beckoning him inside. And behind that man, perhaps being tended to by his kindly wife, a boy sits swaddled in a blanket sipping from a mug of hot chocolate. Cody. His son. Alive.

The tent moves.

Startled, Mike takes a panicked step backward.

Go, if you're going, he tells himself. *The window is closing.*

Body juddering from the force of his own heartbeat, Mike's grip on the walking stick tightens. He looks down to his right, to his flashlight lying forgotten on the ground, the beam directed forward at the tent. He rehearses the steps it will take to grab it and hobble his way out of there through the dark between the trees on the opposite side of the clearing. But then that instinct, so prevalent since first they stumbled upon the clearing, returns, and this time it has a very simple message for him, one he can read as clear as a neon sign through the rain: *Too late.*

Whatever opportunity there might have been up until now, it has passed.

The flashlight is too far away to risk retrieving it. Instead, he unzips one of the pockets in his slicker and plucks out his phone. His hand is trembling so violently, it takes him three tries to hit the ON button. Two seconds later, it glows to life with a hum of vibration and a cheery series of tones that have no place in a situation so grim. A clumsy but hasty series of swipes and button-presses on the rain-smeared screen and he chooses his FLASHLIGHT app, previously only used to help him find dropped items in the car at night, now a potentially life-saving tool in circumstances he doubts the manufacturers ever predicted. The strength of the light as it flares from the back of the phone puts the abandoned flashlight to shame. As he sweeps the blazing blue beam up and out toward the tent, it unveils itself before him, as if it, perhaps possessed by some perverse love for the theatrical, has been waiting for the spotlight to do that very thing.

Mike forgets to breathe as the whole tent flattens and the front folds back like a hood, exposing a pale white triangular shape that might be an angular head with blind, boiled egg eyes. Long thin jaws with curved and curiously blunt yellow teeth snap at the clouds of breath that spume from its narrow throat, and Mike gets another whiff of methane, or perhaps sulfur. The vellum walls of the tent rise up and out before collapsing to the saturated ground with a splash as if abandoning the idea of flight, like kites in a day that has lost its breath. The wings, heavily veined and shaped like those he has seen in illustrations of dragons, now lie flat at right angles to its body, and he can see small thorny nicotine-colored protrusions along the ridge of the wing closest to him. In the center of the creature's mass, beneath its knuckled spine, the skin ripples as something moves beneath it, the same arachnid-like thing he glimpsed in silhouette, the thing that killed his wife. The bulbous light, the lure, pulsates as if in warning, or alarm. For a moment, the cow skull-like head of the creature seems to writhe in protest or in pain, its wings beating clumsily and uselessly at the ground, spattering Mike with rain water. And though he can't be certain of anything given his pedestrian knowledge of such matters, a suspicion floats up through the murk of horror in Mike's mind: He is not looking at one creature, but two, one of them feeding off the other, controlling it. A parasite and its host.

Before he can discover what that parasite might be advising its host to do next, Mike braces himself and allows all the terror, the grief, and the rage to come rushing up from the core of him. The resulting maelstrom of adrenaline is as unknown to him as a foreign language being whispered into his ear, as alien as his enemy, and with a lunatic scream, he closes the distance between them with a series of ungainly steps, and throws himself on top of the flailing creature. He is immediately struck by the fetid stench of the thing and the repulsive feel of its skin against his own. It is like nylon coated in glue and as he scrambles for purchase, tries to dig his nails into its skin, it thrashes beneath him. Struggling not to slide or be thrown free of the creature, thereby losing the only advantage he might get, he brings the walking stick up high, his gaze fixated on the agitated movement in the center of the creature's mass, the engine fueling this horror, the spider-thing that tore his wife from him, and, teeth clenched, brings the stick down with every ounce of strength he has left. It connects with a satisfying crunch, and the skin above it rips, allowing the light to shine through. It is pulsating faster now, and darkening to an orangey-red. The parasite does not make a sound, but wrenches itself away, which has the simultaneous effect of forcing the larger creature to do the same. And when it does, the wing to which Mike clings pulls away, revealing the ground underneath, and any sense of victory he might have felt is quashed as his grip begins to slacken and he begins to slide. Because there *is* no ground underneath, only a deep dark hole, the hole he suspects with mounting horror is the place from which this creature—both of them—came, their ecology forced aboveground perhaps by their own conflict, or hunger, or by man. Such questions will never be answered for Mike, or anyone else, unless these monstrosities grow bolder still and force themselves out further into the world.

He tries to push himself free of the creature, tries to get his feet beneath him, but this, he suspects, is part of the creature's design, a backup plan in case of attack. It has been here for however long, squatting over the hole, safeguarding it, staying close to the only form of egress that makes any sense, while luring in idiot humans.

And how like an idiot Mike feels now as he continues to slide, the foul stench of it filling his nose.

When did it first come? he wonders. *When did it crawl from its subterranean lair, and what did it see when it did? Was it frightened, determined, hungry?* He imagines it waiting in the dark, studying the only other source of light in the dark woods—a yellow tent with a light burning within. Perhaps despite being a creature of the Stygian dark, light is a language it understands. And so it adopts the pose of a tent and sends out its signal in the hope of communicating with this other strange creature. But its only response was to send along the creatures that were hiding inside it. And perhaps once it devoured them, it mulled over the gesture and considered it a gift, for indeed it had been starving.

The creature flails; Mike slips further, hands scrabbling madly for purchase where there is none to be found. The orangey-red light burns crimson. He has wounded the parasite, he's sure of it, but his only reward for his boldness, will be death.

He has time only to pray for a mankind who never knew him that the day will never come in which such creatures grow bold enough to leave this place, and then he is clawing at the wing, thrusting his feet out toward the edges of the ragged hole in one last attempt to save himself, his efforts undone as the creature rises up on its side at the behest of the parasite.

But I did it, Mike thinks, with one single moment of shining pride. *I attacked it, wounded it, maybe killed it. I didn't run. For once, I didn't run.*

There is a brief tantalizing moment in which his fall is halted, the heel of one foot pinned by his own weight and impetus against the grassy edge of the dark hole, his back braced reflexively against the creature's bulk. His mind goes blank. No thoughts, only a flat-line of primal dread laced with acceptance, and a cold electric current that hums through him from groin to sternum, until the parasite bids its host to move again, his foot slips, and the world opens like a hungry mouth beneath him and he is falling.

* * *

The fall seems to last for an eternity, the abyss endless and impenetrably dark. As the air whistles past his ears, he hears first the walking stick, then his phone, splash against the bottom, and is absurdly relieved to know there is one. That there's water suggests he might survive the fall. The odds are not good that he won't simply shatter himself against the rocks, but any odds are better than none.

He is no longer afraid, no longer anything but an empty vessel with one word left on his lips: *Sorry.*

The word is meant for Emma, for Cody, for himself, until he has the opportunity to tell them face to face in whatever follows oblivion, assuming anything does.

The promise of it gives him a smile.

Sixty feet down, a tall thin stalagmite abruptly halts his descent, punching through his stomach, shattering his lower vertebrae, and suspending him there in the dark like a fly on a needle. The pain feels like something bestowed upon someone else. He is already dying, finally ready to exit a world that was Not His Department.

Soon, his beloved mother comes and mercifully mutes the world for her little boy, one last time.

* * *

On the opposite side of the clearing, unexplored by Mike or his ill-fated wife, the hill slopes downward through another two miles of dense, tangled woodland. A disused and therefore untrustworthy slatted wooden rope-bridge crosses a narrow river which, if followed south for another quarter-mile, leads to the approved camping ground Mike eschewed despite the camp attendant's instructions.

As the sun rises on the new day like a swollen, burning pumpkin, turning to sparkling diamonds the beads of water left in the wake of the storm and coaxing veils of mist up from the sodden earth, Greg Kohl, a fifty-three year old college lecturer, emerges from his tent and stretches. Refreshed despite a sleep frequently interrupted by volleys of thunder and the howling wind, he sets about making coffee for himself and his girlfriend, Karen, a girl who is thirty years his junior, a revelation in the sack, and the third girl he has brought up here in the past ten months. With no one to answer to up here but his own ego, he permits himself a satisfied grin, and, as he sets up the camp stove, replays the memory of Karen's nubile body, and the various creative ways in which she let him use it.

When he realizes there is a kid standing less than two feet away from him, he starts, almost burns himself on the camp stove and curses, then, as he takes in the face of his visitor, immediately wishes he hadn't.

The kid looks like something from a documentary about the Serbian war. His clothes are caked in mud and soaking wet, as if he spent the night in the woods, in the rain. He is shivering violently, his teeth making audible clicking sounds. In the oval of his dirty face, his eyes are wide, the pupils amid the blue shrunken down to pinpoints. The kid has his arms down by his sides, the index fingers of both hands tapping against his palms, as if he thinks he's playing a videogame.

"Hey," Greg says, and rises. "You okay, kid?"

It's a ridiculous question, because clearly the kid isn't, but he's not sure what else to say. Greg swallows, tries to think, something that's never easy for him in the pre-coffee stages of his mornings, and especially with the hangover that's pounding against the walls of his skull like a lunatic inmate. But something is wrong here. The kid before him looks the very definition of haunted, so he knows he has to do something, become the conscientious, helpful adult, even though he'd rather just crawl back inside the tent and curl up beside the lovely Karen Wilkes.

"What's your name?" he asks, because that seems as good a place to start as any.

The kid just stands there, lips dry and cracked and sealed like a scar, watching him.

"Did something happen?" Another dumb question, but Greg is at a loss. So he raises a finger, as if he has lost his voice too, or as if he thinks the child might respond better to non-verbalized communication, indicating that the kid should wait, and he ducks back inside the tent. It reeks of sex, stale perfume, and alcohol. Karen, little more than a tangle of blonde hair on her inflatable pillow, moans and rolls over, squints up at him, her mascara smudged around her eyes, making her look significantly less attractive than he found her last night. Her sleeping bag is wrapped tightly around her, but there's no missing the half-moons of her large, surgically enhanced breasts over the material. It's the first time he's been with someone who has fake breasts, and he does not consider himself a fan. Wild horses could not drag that admission out of him, however, for Greg is a man who is thankful for the women his charm and money and position of authority affords him, particularly in light of his ugly, and ongoing, marital dissolution.

"What's going on?" she mumbles, throwing a hand with French-manicured fingernails over her eyes.

"I need a blanket," Greg tells her. "Some kid's in trouble."

"Trouble?"

"Yeah. Go back to sleep. I'll take care of it."

"And then me?" She smiles sleepily, another hint of the neediness she has been displaying on and off since they violated the teacher-student rule and became an item.

"Yeah, and you," he promises, and yanks the spare blanket off her.

"Boo. So cold," she says, and rolls over.

Ever the humanitarian, Greg thinks, and exits the tent.

The kid is right where he left him, still standing there shivering and looking shell-shocked. Greg can't help wondering about the nature of his ordeal. Was he in a car crash? Get lost in the woods? See something terrible? Or is he just some local yokel's kid, wandered down out of the mountains to bug the regular folk for money or food. The theme song to *Deliverance* twangs through his head and he has to struggle to suppress a smile.

"Here kid," he says and holds the blanket up to indicate his intent.

The kid backs away. Greg stops, frowns.

"You're freezing. Let me put the blanket on you and we'll get you some coffee and figure out what to do next, okay?"

The kid gives no sign that he understands, which leads Greg to the conclusion that whatever the boy has been through, it was pretty bad. He decides the best course of action after getting the kid warm, is to get to the camping office down the trail and either wait for the attendant to show, or see if there's an emergency number he can call. Someone has to be looking for the kid, after all.

Again he tries to swoop the blanket like a cape around the kid's shoulders, and almost manages it this time, one half of it coming down on the backpack that's slung over the boy's shoulders. But as soon as the material hits the pack, the kid winces and backs away. It is the first sign of emotion the child has shown, and it alarms Greg, who takes it as an indication that the boy is wounded. After a moment of indecision, he lets the blanket fall to the ground.

"Okay," he says. "Will you let me take a look? If you're hurt, I might be able to help."

How he might be able to help when his area of expertise is

American History is anybody's guess, but he needs to get the kid to trust him, to let him at least gauge the extent of the trouble he, and by association, Greg, is in.

"Easy now." As he starts to move slowly and carefully toward the boy, hands raised to show he means no harm, he finds himself surprised at the situation in which he has found himself, for while he's reluctant to call himself a selfish man, the last few years of his life have definitely seen him dedicating the lion's share of his efforts to pursuits designed solely to benefit nobody but himself. Call it the fallout from a life spent trying to be fair and equal, with little reward. That he didn't immediately try to slough the responsibility for this kid off on someone, *any*one else, or just go back into the tent and zip it up when he first encountered him, is certainly not in keeping with his character. *My good deed for the day*, he decides.

A quick look around at the campsite reveals that all but one of the other couples have already packed up and left, and the only sign of life from the remaining tent is a soft, droning snore. Greg wonders if he should rouse the other couple. He recalls the wife being pretty hot too, even if she was closer to his age and showing every last bit of it. The husband was a quiet type, so maybe the wife might be impressed by Greg's heroics and therefore amenable to a little three-way extramarital fun with Synthetic Karen, assuming they could find a way to get rid of hubby for a while.

Jesus, he tells himself. *What's the matter with you?*

With a grin, he shakes his head. *The age old question, hombre, but what fun it is pursuing the answer.*

The kid is close enough for him to touch now, and stiffens, raises his shoulders. Head bowed, he looks up at Greg from beneath a furrowed brow and the ragged theater wings of his damp hair.

"I'm not going to hurt you," Greg tells him. "I promise. But if you're hurt, I want to help you, understand?"

Again, no indication from the boy that he understands anything, but despite his defensive posture, he does not move away this time, and Greg takes that as a positive sign. He slowly moves around the boy, inspecting his neck for bruises or wounds, and sees nothing but fish-belly white skin, the shivering intensifying.

"There's nothing to be afraid of," Greg says in the same comforting, disarming tone he uses to such great effect on his dates. The backpack is covered in a thick layer of slowly drying mud, the weight of which goes some way toward explaining the discomfort on the child's face when the blanket touched it. God knows how far the poor kid trekked with all that crap on his back.

"First things first," he says, "Let's get this thing off you."

The kid goes rigid, turns to stone, but Greg figures it's now or never and quickly grabs the sides of the backpack, intending to lift it up to relieve the boy of his burden.

A moment of confusion as the backpack, much heavier than he anticipated, moves liquidly beneath Greg's fingers, as if he has grabbed a slimy bag of fish, and he grimaces as the mud begins to slough off around and through his fingers. Repulsed as he is, he decides it is better to keep going. Dropping something this heavy back down on the kid's back might send him sprawling. That would be the perfect time for the other couple to poke their heads out of the tent, wouldn't it? *Hey*, he imagines them yelling at him, *leave that poor kid alone*.

"Jesus," he hisses through his teeth. "What have you got in here, kid, rocks?"

An inch from the boy's flesh, and the backpack snags on something, something that resists Greg's efforts, and no matter how hard he pulls, it refuses to yield to him.

The boy lowers his head further, begins to sob, and Greg feels a rush of guilt.

I'm hurting him. I should just—

It is at that moment that he catches of glimpse of what's holding the pack in place. It's something black and knuckled, like a long, thin, spindly twig, and it appears to be buried in the boy's shoulder.

More of the mud slides off, splattering Greg's shoes. He doesn't notice.

"What the fuck?" he asks, forgetting himself, as he hoists up the other side of the backpack as far as it will go, as much as it will let him, and notes another of the black knuckled sticks on that side too, the length of it seeming to sprout from the pack into a raw red puncture wound on the boy's back, connecting one to the other.

The backpack moves, and with a cry of fright, Greg releases it, and watches the boy stagger forward a step before its weight.

"I don't know…" Greg says, appalled. "I just…what the hell is that thing, kid?"

His mind floods with images of child torturers and abusive

parents, of weird cults, and maniacs, and still he shakes his head. He has been alive for half a century and has never encountered anything like this.

And then he notices something hanging from the underside of the backpack, at the small of the boy's back. At first glimpse it appears to be a water vessel of some kind, but it looks too fleshy for that, and although he has no problem admitting that there is a lot he doesn't know about the world, one thing he's pretty sure of is that canteens don't glow, or look like plant bulbs. And as he watches, his hand straying to his brow as if to contain his confusion, the light begins to pulsate.

First: amber.

The child's shuddering worsens.

Then orange.

The boy falls to his knees as the backpack, presented with a more formidable, mature, and therefore infinitely more useful host, begins to detach itself with the sound of a Velcro strap being torn away.

Then red.

And Greg Kohl, who has spent his last few years looking out only for himself, abruptly finds himself in service to another.

* * *

Forty-five minutes later, Danielle Miller, the camp attendant, arrives at work with a hangover that would have rivaled Greg Kohl's in potency. And like the recently *appropriated* Mr. Kohl, Danielle's thoughts are fixated this day on her partner, namely the girl she will, this coming weekend, be bringing to meet her folks for the first time. She suspects her mother will be shocked, but understanding, when she learns of her precious daughter's sexual preference. She suspects her father will disown her. But the time for hiding, for lying and pretending she's something she is not, and never has been, is over. And if the cost of liberation and honesty is the love of her father, then so be it. It will just mean that all those years of him claiming he would love her no matter what she did in life will make him the liar.

She pulls into the parking lot and kills the engine, sits for a moment in the stillness which is always her favorite part of the day. This is her second year working here, and so perhaps she no longer appreciates the beauty of the area as much as she once did, as others do, but she will always appreciate the quiet. Particularly today when she knows her bold claims about her father are not entirely true. She loves him, and always will. And she knows he loves her too. She just wants more than anything for him to surprise her, to support her, to let them all move on as if nothing's changed, because for Danielle, they haven't.

She steps out of the car and grabs the brown bag containing the lunch Erica packed for her. The contents thrill her not at all. She'd much rather a double cheeseburger and fries from the nearby Wendy's than the turkey wrap and kale chips, but they have a dieting pact and she's determined not to be the first one to cave. She'll still be starving afterward, but isn't that the point of a diet?

With a slight smile at the image of her beautiful Erica chastising her for her thoughts of insubordination, she slams the car door, noting the presence of the old Toyota among the few vehicles remaining in the lot, and lets herself into the office. As it always has since it was first built, it smells of freshly cut timber, a smell she adores. Tossing her unappealing lunch on the chipped and scarred table, she goes to the window that grants a view of the trail and the camping ground at the crest of the hill.

She prays today of all days that she won't have to listen to the campers bitching about last night's storm, as if she could have done anything to prevent it.

Then her heart sinks as a gust of wind across the campsite sends fallen material waving to her like a red hand.

Shit. Of the two tents remaining in camp, one has fallen, victim, she assumes, of the storm. With a sigh of irritation, she realizes her hope that the owners left in the night as soon as the going got rough was a naïve one. She did warn them of the impending storm, after all. Told them it might be better to come back tomorrow. But those owners, a perv professor and his girlfriend—who looked young enough to be his daughter—clearly had other things on their minds to be bothered by such trivial things as caution.

She's about to move away from the window when, as if summoned by her thoughts of him, down the trail comes the creepy professor, the one who looked at her like a starving man looks at a rotisserie chicken when he checked in, his bespectacled eyes addressing her breasts as if they were doing the talking. He is disheveled and wearing what looks like a large muddy backpack, the weight of it clearly affecting his balance.

"Great," she groans, encouraged even less by the stilted walk and pallid face of the man as he clomps his way toward the office, his expression like a man who has just received the worst kind of news. *Probably still drunk.*

What she cannot yet see from her limited viewpoint are the small, faintly glowing, egg-like sores that are already beginning to surface around the professor's throat. When she does register them, she will assume they are burns sustained from some kind of accident. She will only realize her mistake when those boils pop and send their contents into her eyes and open mouth.

And Danielle will forget her diet in favor of a whole different kind of sustenance.

"So much for a hassle-free day," she murmurs to herself, as she scoops up her keys and goes out to meet the professor.

* * *

In the pool at the bottom of the shaft dug by the creature at the behest of its puppeteer, its winged, flightless, dragon-like brethren swim in crude circles, blind and oblivious to the presence of the dead man impaled upon the stalagmite above them, but excited by the blood that rains down from Up There, a place the parasites attached to their undersides tell them they will one day visit for themselves…

…while Up There, Greg the professor and Danielle, no longer driven by compulsions of their own, sit into their respective vehicles and shut the doors. They wait. Soon after, they are joined by the Professor's girlfriend, and the couple from the other tent: Stan and Marcy Hopkins, all of them called to the parking lot by the parasite, all of them wearing faintly glowing necklaces of the creature's incubating spawn. For a while none of them do anything but sit stock-still and listen to their new and merciless internal voices. Occasionally pain flickers across their faces as the parasite punishes their attempts to resist its influence, secreting painful toxins into their bloodstream until once more they are forced to obey, and rewarding them with brief surges of endorphins when they do.

At length, and in perfect synchronicity, bidden by commands clearer to them than the voices of their own muted consciences, the egg sacs pulsing brighter as the creature nourishes its young in preparation for the hatching, Danielle, Greg, and Stan start up their vehicles and slowly reverse out of the campground parking lot.

Beyond the narrow lanes and the twisting mountain roads, the city awaits, unaware of the alien threat that will soon infect its veins.

The parasite shivers in anticipation as they clear the shadow of the mountain it has called home for a hundred thousand years.

YOU IN?

YOU IN?

Almost midnight.

To the man standing in the snow, shoulders hunched against the cold, it seemed ironic that Abigail Point Securicorp, a company dedicated to the prevention of theft, should choose to leave the keys to the inn outside their office doors rather than in a lockbox somewhere. They really hadn't even made much of an effort to hide them. Anyone passing might notice the large white padded envelope bearing the name PETER HASKINS propped up against the glass to the right of the office door, and he hardly thought the small layer of snow on the window ledge provided adequate camouflage. Still, as he shuddered away the attention of an icy gust that ran cold fingers up his spine and scalp, he supposed if they hadn't worried about it, then he shouldn't either. Besides, no matter how questionable their methods, or untrustworthy some of the nocturnal wanderers in Abigail Point might be, the keys *were* here. No one had seen fit to snatch them, and for that Peter was eternally grateful. The way his luck was going, he had fully expected to arrive at the office to find the keys gone, only a small rectangular pocket in the snow a sign that they'd ever been there. Of course, had that been the case, he could have called his new boss, or taken it upon himself to hurry to the Wickerwood Inn to confront the thief, but for a guy with Peter's reputation, the former course of action would undoubtedly lead his employer to suspect he'd taken the keys himself, perhaps to use at a later date to break into the hotel, while the latter represented more risk than he was willing to deal with on his own.

He shook his head. It didn't matter. Securicorp had given him the job, and the keys were where they'd left them. It was a good sign, an indication perhaps that almost eight months of dismal luck were finally coming to an end.

His reflection in the glass made a thin, pale-faced specter of him as he reached for the envelope. Snow left wet kisses on his wrist, the misty clouds of his breath billowing around him as he transferred the keys, still inside the envelope, into his pocket, following them with a cold hand to ensure they didn't somehow escape him on the short walk to the Wickerwood.

* * *

In daylight the Victorian and Italianate houses along Stanton Street stared proudly out over Abigail Point Harbor with spines straight as a Civil War General's, their windows gleaming like battle-hardened eyes on the verge of weeping at the sight of home. Tonight, however, as Peter bowed his head against the frigid wind, the moonless night had robbed those painted ladies of their luster, making them notable only by the weight of their timeless silhouettes and the faintest sparkle on their ice-limned balustrades.

The street was quiet, the cars parked on both sides silent beneath skins of frost. The faintest hush could be heard from the sea, punctuated here and there by the abrasive cry of a gull and the echo of Peter's footfalls. Lonesome sounds, that made him feel like the only man in town not invited to a party.

He huffed breath into the lapels of his coat and pressed the warmth to his face as he thought of the newspaper ad that had led him here. *Night Security Wanted for the Wickerwood Inn, November 20th - 27th. 12. a.m. - 6. a.m. $400 p.w.*

Four-hundred bucks for a week of watching over machinery and tools. He could hardly believe it, no more than he could believe someone had bought the Wickerwood Inn again. He would have thought, after all the unpleasant things rumored to have gone on there, that people would have learned to let it be. Not that he really gave much credence to that kind of nonsense, though he found it a lot easier to scoff at from the comfort of his sunlit living room than he did making his merry way in the freezing cold to spend the night in it. But even if it had been scientifically proven to him that the incidents at the inn had been caused by something other than poor luck, the money would have kept him moving briskly toward it. There was the cold, for one, and he'd been told there was a construction heater awaiting him in the lobby. For another, there were the debts, haunting him with a tenacity that would put any ghost to shame. And above all other considerations, there was Claire.

He closed his eyes, briefly, and there she was, as if the ice crystals had projected her likeness onto his retinas. Claire. The one person, perhaps the *last* person who still had faith in him, still believed he could make something of himself. If not for her, he'd still be operating under the delusion that gambling was a form of employment, the casino his workplace, every paycheck dependent on the capricious Fates. She'd saved him from that, took him in, loved him, and asked only that he *try*.

Try to find a good job, a real job.

Try to stop being a creature whose probable future was a direct result of his being unable to let go of an unsavory past, a man who based every decision on the allure of certain numbers and the quality of the light on any given Friday in Atlantic City.

And because he loved her, and because he couldn't remember ever being as happy as she made him, he did try, and the effort he made was so uncharacteristically ardent, so substantial and heartfelt, it made his eventual failure all the more devastating for them both. She hadn't kicked him out, even after almost six months of false starts: jobs he took only to lose or get fired from; get-rich quick schemes that nosedived and made him more enemies than friends; half-baked strategies that were smothered at birth. No, she hadn't kicked him out, because of her unshakeable belief that it would work out in the end. And it wasn't until she said those words --*it'll work out in the end, Pete*--while sweeping up the glass that lay scattered around a rock someone--undoubtedly one of the many bookies he had been desperately avoiding--had hurled through their living room window, that he saw the end coming. Because it wasn't the first rock someone had thrown through his window. The last one, some years before, had had his surname (minus the final 's') written on it in black marker, which he didn't see until the policeman held it up in front of his face, Pete's eight-month-old son's blood still dripping from it, and the child's mother, Alison, screaming hysterically and clawing to get at him from somewhere amid the chaos of lights and noise.

As he turned onto Jericho Street, leaving Stanton behind him, he thought of the envelope in his pocket, his name scrawled across it in black ink. If it had been stolen, the thief would have been taking more than just a bunch of keys. They'd have robbed him of his chance to finally start making things right, to prove himself to Claire.

And now that someone else had finally decided to take a chance on him, namely the sour-faced manager of Abigail Point Securicorp, he intended to make good on it, to repay Claire for her faith, and her love.

Tonight, in the abandoned shell of the Wickerwood Inn, he would begin renovations of his own.

* * *

The aesthetic contradiction of a white picket fence around a Southern Gothic manor, built in the style of a paddlewheel riverboat, hadn't been lost on the youths of Abigail Point, who had, at some point in the year and a half the inn had been closed, kicked away the posts and slats until it looked like the broken grin of a beaten drunk. The construction crew, or perhaps more discerning vandals, had made off with the flat marbled stones which in their prime had led from the small gate up a short incline to the main door, leaving behind an unimaginative hopscotch game as the only viable path through an explosion of undergrowth. Unlike the painted ladies on Stanton Street, Wickerwood Inn, standing tall and silent above the verdant frenzy, did not stare out to sea or glare at the statue of the Civil War general in the park across the street, but the darkness lent it by the plywood boards shoved rudely into its glassless frames. Opaque sheets of plastic snapped and fluttered in the wind from windows on the second and third floors; the cupola seemed to totter from its place on the fourth. Verandas framed every floor and appeared spacious now that the rocking chairs--favored by the guests no matter what the weather--were gone. As Peter stood there, drawing out the keys, he thought the faint sigh of the tide could just as easily have been Wickerwood's labored breathing; it certainly looked like a sickly old man in a new suit, sagging inside but presenting the best face it could to anyone watching, which only made its appearance all the more pitiful.

The jingle of the keys hitting his palm was a reassuringly *normal* sound as Peter slipped them from the envelope. He had never been this close to the inn before, and never this late, when the ordinary ambience of a bustling seaside town wasn't there to drown out the creaks and groans and shudders of a building slouching beneath the weight of abandonment; when the sunlight wasn't there to burn away shadows that seemed to sprout and grow the longer he looked upon the monolithic aspect of the house; when the wind entered the cracks and fissures in the building and emerged as voices. He understood better then, as he lingered on the threshold of the property, the ease with which the house had gained its dark reputation. Whether justified or not, it certainly looked the part.

A quick check of his watch told him he'd been dawdling at the gate for almost eight minutes, and while he would have been surprised (and more than a little startled) to find someone from Securicorp waiting inside the house to chide him for his tardiness, it made no sense to stay out in the bitter cold any longer. With one final look over his shoulder at the quiet, empty street, he sighed and stepped onto the path.

* * *

After a further five minutes spent wrestling with the heavy, slightly rusted padlock that hung like a medallion from the chains looped through and around the front door's thick brass handles, there was a dull but satisfying click and Peter watched as the chains spilled to the floor, the rattling of the steel links through the handles more noise than he had encountered all night. He winced, realizing that though the Wickerwood's neighbors were a fair distance away, at this time of night the clamor he had just made had nothing to compete with and so would carry unfiltered to their ears. They might assume he was breaking in, and call the cops, who would know Peter only as a troublemaker they'd had dealings with in the past. The fact that beneath his overcoat he was wearing the dark blue Securicorp uniform, complete with clip-on tie and the company's gold insignia emblazoned on the breast would mean nothing. They'd assume he stole that too. He'd be tossed in jail until they confirmed that his claims were true. And that would be enough to make his boss think hiring him had been a mistake. Once again his past would intrude on the present, ruining his chance to make good.

Dispirited at the bleak reminder of just how easy his best intentions could be derailed, he carefully picked up the chains and set them aside so they were not blocking the door. Pocketing the padlock, he picked through the keys until he found a slim silver one, the initials WW ornately suspended within the oval bow, and slid it into the lock. To his surprise, it turned with a fluidity that suggested recent oiling, and the door caught only once before swinging open.

* * *

He'd forgotten to bring the flashlight.

Inside the building, with little illumination from the open doorway at his back, and a mass of jagged shadows scattered before him, he cursed his forgetfulness. He was told there would be heat and light, and he believed there would be, but to get to appliances that would bestow these luxuries upon him, he would have to stumble around in the dark, and God only knew what might be scattered about on the floor between here and there.

"Nice job, Pete." This self-admonition sounded very small, very alone, and completely devoid of conviction. It compelled him to get moving.

With his hands held out before him like antennae, he felt his way through the dark, the smell of dust and mold making his nose tickle. Shuffling, he stumbled when his shoes rammed against obstructions too heavy to yield before his passage or tangled in treacherous snares of plastic sheeting, and had to restrain a howl of pain when he banged his knee against something hard and cold. Glassy pain spread over the offended joint. Steadying himself, and with sparks dancing across his field of vision, he muttered a curse to Lady Luck and all her departure from his life had cost him.

Nah, he told himself a few moments later, as the pain dulled to a warm throb in his kneecap, *forgetting the damn flashlight was all you, buddy*. Eventually, by using hands and feet to probe the surfaces ahead of him, like a man walking on unsteady ice, he found one of the lamps, and quickly felt for the button that would chase away the increasingly treacherous dark.

A click, and the room flooded with light, blinding him. He stumbled back a step, blinking furiously until his back met resistance, which he then used to maintain his balance in the seemingly crowded room.

Turning his head away from the light, he waited for his vision to clear. When at last it did, what he saw made him forget about the other lamps, and the heater. Instead it made him think of Claire.

She had been working as a waitress in the Tropicana Hotel in Atlantic City when they'd first met. It was there she'd defied all his expectations and inflamed his belief in Lady Luck by approaching him before he'd even worked up the nerve to look her way a second time. The first night they shared a bed, she'd told him about her plans to move to Abigail Point, to "leave behind the sleaze for a place where the air doesn't stink of desperation and dirty money" was how she'd put it. She'd shown him a brochure, designed by the Abigail Point Tourism Office to seduce outsiders into its folds. Among the pretty pictures of Victorian manors, glistening beaches and lofty lighthouses, there'd been interior shots of the Wickerwood Inn in all its opulent glory--a vibrant, proud place, from the gleaming crystal of the expensive chandeliers in the Rosewind restaurant, to the crisp and simple elegance of its rooms.

But the building in which Peter now stood was not elegant. It was a wreck. The lobby floor was covered in debris: splintered wood, cracked stone blocks, ruined furniture, broken glass and garbage, all of which merely served as a carpet to help obscure the badly damaged parquet underneath. Here was an old oak door, laid catty-corner on its side, three of the four stained-glass insets shattered, leaving emerald and crimson-colored teeth poking from the frames. Here, a stack of screens, badly ripped; here, a cart loaded with linens that had once been white but were now so dusty they'd turned gray; there a mountain of cardboard boxes growing in a corner and held together by large scabrous patches of mold.

At the head of the room, directly opposite the front door, was a surprisingly undamaged and new-looking registration desk. Upon it sat a cordless drill, a spool of extension cord, a crumpled pack of Pall Malls and a dusty bell.

Peter sidestepped the crusty maw of a cement mixer, which his new found sense of direction told him had been the object he'd collided with earlier. A few feet away stood another halogen lamp, its thick glass face turned toward the ropy mess of wires that hung from the ceiling where once there had been a light. To the right of it, looking like the turbine of a small jet engine set atop a cannon mount, was the construction heater.

He slid the keys back into his pocket, where their weight crumpled the now empty envelope. As he edged his way toward the heater via a crooked aisle of toolboxes, concrete blocks and what appeared to be a twine-bound bundle of yellowed newspaper, the tips of his fingers tingling at the thought of warmth, someone laughed.

Peter jumped, but did not stop moving. He was too cold for that. But he slowed his pace, his spine rigid, the hair on the back of his neck rising until the sensation was almost painful. Without turning to face the direction in which the laugh had come, he dropped his gaze to one of the toolboxes at his feet. *Plenty of weapons there*, he thought, and tried to swallow the knot of fear that had abruptly sucked the moisture from his mouth. *Should have known. Nothing's easy.*

He reached the heater and moved around it, so that the front door was behind him, the small entryway to the hall directly ahead, and waited for the sound to come again. Finger poised on the switch that would flood the room with much-needed heat, he stared through the clouds of his breath at the oblong of darkness to the right of the registration desk, the portal from which the sound of mirth had rolled like dust from an old closet.

A light came on.

He flinched so hard his finger jabbed the switch and the heater rumbled into life, startling him even more. Reminded of his boss's caveat, *Stand too close to that thing and you'll be well done within a half-minute*, he quickly backed away toward the front door and out of the range of the heater's mouth. "Damn it." He ran a hand through his coarse hair, and weighed his options. *It's just kids, probably*, he thought, but didn't believe it. The laugh had had a wheezing quality to it, better suited to an old man with emphysema than some punk kid. *But for Chrissakes, there isn't supposed to be* anyone *here, so what difference does it make who--*

His thoughts were interrupted by movement in the hall. Someone had passed in front of the light source in there, sending a lithe shadow sprawling toward the lobby where Peter stood paralyzed by indecision. "Hey," he yelled, fear shoving the word out of him before he knew it was coming. Quickly, he dropped to his haunches and grabbed a well-used hammer from atop one of the toolboxes. The heft of it in his palm made him feel a little better. The thought of what he might be forced to do with it, didn't. He rose on unsteady legs.

And: "Hey ya'self," a voice answered.

* * *

Fear gave way to confusion. He was supposed to be alone. They had told him he would be. Ergo, whoever was calling and casting shadows from somewhere down the hall was an intruder. Simple as that.

Only it wasn't.

Peter had taken the job, despite being briefed on the possible risks. He'd nodded in all the right places, kept his jaw set and his back straight to compliment the verbal assurances to his employer that he was the man for the job, no matter what. But in his mind he'd been grinning. Wickerwood was a battered old ruin, held up not by joists and walls but by reputation and respect, boarded up and locked to keep its secrets within and those who sought to know them without. He'd expected to sit on the stairs in the heat, reading the battered old Ed McBain paperback he'd crammed into his inside pocket while he tuned out the old protests of an ancient building. He'd expected to sleep most of the way toward some easy money. What he hadn't expected was to find himself frozen in the lobby, desperately trying to remember what his boss had told him to do in the "unlikely" event that he discovered he wasn't alone.

Whatever that advice, that training, had been, was now proving just as elusive as the source of the disembodied voice. He hadn't listened, hadn't cared. He'd been thinking of the money.

His grip tightened on the hammer.

Leave, said a mental voice he wasn't entirely sure had been offered by his own brain. It had almost seemed to come from over his shoulder, and the flesh on his back tightened. He thought of turning to look-- *Just my luck to stumble into a friggin' ambush*--but more laughter stopped him, jarring him worse than before because this time it was not just one voice, but many. To Peter, it was the once familiar sound of a bunch of friends sharing a laugh over a private joke.

Private joke. Private party.

An overwhelming sense of alienation washed over him. In there, somewhere, lounging in the shadows of the hall, were people, a bunch of guys by the sound of it, and their very presence made him feel as useless as he had always suspected he was. He'd tried to make something of himself, was *still* trying, but as per goddamn usual, every opportunity came with a built-in peanut gallery. Anger coursed through him. The rubber on the handle of the hammer squeaked beneath his tightening grip. His knuckles turned white. He was so tired of this. So tired of the odds always being stacked against him, tired of being the guy left to skulk out the door on a wave of someone else's laughter...of being the guy in the lobby listening to the mirth from the lounge. Well to hell with it; he wasn't leaving. Though the decision made unease thrum through him, knowing it was final imbued him with confidence, however frail. He squared his shoulders, ignored the imagined whisper--"mistake"--that drifted over his shoulder and called out, "This is security. Who's back there? There's no one supposed to be in here," in as authoritative a tone as he could muster.

The silence that came back to him was thick and endless, and it allowed the single most crucial bit of truth to settle in Peter's mind: *There are more of them than you*, before he broke it himself. "Hey, you hear me? You got five m--"

"Quit yer damn screamin'," a voice interrupted, sounding no closer than it had before. "Louie's still hungover."

Winos.

Peter closed his eyes and let some of the tension drain from his shoulders, though his grip on the hammer did not loosen. Drunks he could handle, even if they reacted somewhat belligerently to his attempts to roust them. And hell, maybe he'd even leave them alone; let them sleep in the house. What did he care? During what felt like an eternal spell of rotten luck, Peter had more than once found himself with an old coat as a bed sheet, a park bench as a bed, and while he was loathe to compare himself in any way to a bunch of tramps, he nonetheless felt sympathy for them. It was going to be a long night. As long as he shunted them out before dawn and relief came, nobody would be any the wiser.

He allowed himself a wan smile and made his way toward the hall. "You guys aren't supposed to be roosting in here," he said, but with less authority than before. "This building could come down around your ears. That, or the cops."

"Eh, we own those fucks," a voice replied, and Peter's smile vanished as he reached the doorway. Beyond it, the air was considerably colder. *That doesn't sound like a wino*, he thought. *Far too sober. Far too cocky.* His eyes settled on the dim yellow orb of light at the far end of the hall. An old hurricane lamp had been lit and set on the floor between the last door on the left side of the hall, and the one on the right. Further illumination came from the latter. Faintly glowing smoke breathed out into the musty air.

They would have lit a fire to keep them warm, he told himself, but immediately countered the thought with: *Why, when they had the use of the heaters?*

More laughter, then someone cursed and the laughter doubled. It was followed by a horribly familiar sound, a sound that had featured as much in Peter's dreams as it had in his most feverish nightmares. A sound that might as well have been the turning of a key to the forbidden area of Peter's mind, to a door behind which ghosts and demons clawed for release. Gooseflesh rippled his skin, every hair feeling like needles stabbed into his arm. The haze in the hall began to smell like cigar smoke. Panic returned and despite the chill, perspiration broke out all over his body.

No.

"Think he'll wanna?" someone asked.

"Damn right he will," someone else replied.

"Who's there?" Peter asked, but did not receive an answer.

He sagged against the doorframe.

Leave now.

But he couldn't, despite every particle of his being trying its damndest to propel him out of there.

He swallowed, squeezed his eyes shut and tried to picture Claire but her face was condensation on glass, running and melting in his memory.

"Shit." He rubbed the palm of his free hand over his face and it came away wet. *Okay, man, keep it together. You're getting way too bent out of shape over this. Something to prove, right? So prove something.*

"Hey Security. You in or out?"

The sound came again--*snick!*--and it was a leash that tugged at Peter, trying to jerk him into the hall, over the threshold of fear and toward the light. The hammer slipped from his sweaty grip and thumped to the floor. He bent down to retrieve it and a sudden horrid stench rose from the knotted red fibers of the carpet, as if he'd dunked his head in a cold river of sewage. It stuffed his nose, reached down his throat with foul fingers and he gagged, tried to rise, but the hall jerked away from him, the hurricane lamp a long fat splash of color that streaked across his vision.

Abruptly, there were people in the hall with him.

He could see them in his peripheral vision, staring at him. The laughing men, maybe? He squinted, trying to focus. No, it wasn't. Men, women and children, and not a single one of them looked capable of laughter. Some of them brushed long-fingered hands over old fashioned dresses, others held hats clutched to their chests in a gesture of respect that did not match the malice on their faces. He thought one might have been holding a limbless doll; another a straw hat with dark splotches on the brim. Still another held a whip, hanging limp like a dead snake. A silent crowd, all waiting for something. They could have been portraits, such was the motionless intensity of their presence, and he had no doubt they wished him harm. He put a hand to his temple and tried to massage sanity back into the scene, and when next he looked upon it, the people were gone.

Dizzy, disorientated, unsure from which direction he had come, he put a hand against the leprous yellow wallpaper and it moved beneath his hand. He jerked away and studied the spot where his hand had been. The impossibly sized cockroach or spider his imagination had told him had been there wasn't. There was nothing but mildewed wall.

"Hey? You still out there, Mac?"

"Fuck this," Pete muttered. He was going to get the hell out of Dodge while he still had his health. He'd go home, get some sleep, and tomorrow he could look for another job, something that didn't involve weird old inns, toxic fumes and cackling winos.

You're high from whatever shit they sprayed on that carpet, that's all. He agreed. Maybe the men in the room were high too, and that's why they were laughing so much.

They're laughing because they're having a good time.

He turned, nausea whirling through him, threatening to send him back to the carpet where he would most certainly die from inhaling whatever chemicals had saturated it.

"Pussying out?"

Slowly, Pete looked back toward the light and the room, and there was a man standing there, a figure utterly unlike the people he thought he'd seen a few moments ago. For one, he was smiling. For another, he did not vanish when Pete looked straight at him.

Exhausted, dispirited, and unnerved, Pete ignored the insult. "Who the hell are you?"

The stranger took a long puff from his Cuban cigar and tilted his head back to aim a jet of smoke at the ceiling. When he was done admiring the fog he'd created, he shrugged and licked his thin lips. "A friend," he said. "And we're one man short. You in?"

"What are you doing here? No one's supposed to be here."

The man was dressed in an expensive gray suit, complimented by a dark red tie and charcoal-colored hat. The lamplight gleamed on the polished surface of his shoes, and the gold ring on the index finger curled around his cigar. "Hey, so what, right? So no one's supposed to be here. But we are, and figure if we gotta be here then we may as well pass the time somehow, right?"

"I have to go," Peter said, sick at the feeble sound of his own voice, and started to turn.

"I know you," the man said.

"What?" Peter did not look over his shoulder.

"I know you."

"How?"

"Well..." The man chuckled. "Not you personally, at least, not yet I don't. What I mean is...ah shit, I ain't so good at expressin' it, y'know? Not like Frankie is. He's our college boy." He sighed heavily.

Peter waited.

At length the man made a satisfied grunt. "I know your *type*. That's it."

Don't rise to the bait, Peter told himself, just keep moving. *If he aims to stop you, he's too far away to catch you before you make the door.* The words came to him sluggishly through a mist of pain and confusion that robbed them of their immediacy. "And what's my 'type'?" he asked, turning back to face the man.

The man's wide grin made him look predatory, shark-like. "A loser."

Peter straightened his posture and tried to make himself look as imposing as possible, a task made harder by the dizziness and the feeling as if he'd already taken a beating. *What the hell was on that carpet?* But any worries he might have had about the effect of toxins on his health were set aside in favor of defending what little honor he had left. "What did you call me?"

The man gestured with his cigar, scribbling smoke in the air before him. "No offense, Mac. I don't mean it as an insult."

"Then explain it."

"Aw c'mon. Don't go gettin' riled up now. We're just talkin' here, right?"

Peter didn't answer. He glared.

"What I meant was that you seem to be a guy who's spent most of his life trying to turn his luck around but somehow always ends up on his ass. Not that it's your fault. Hell," he chuckled, "I've been there. Most of my boys been there at some stage. Happens to the best of us. You put all your faith in somethin' and it turns rotten. What can you do, right? S'all I was saying."

"Huh." Peter shook his head. "You don't know the first thing about me."

"Sure I do." The man's eyes sparkled. He took a puff on his cigar, and let the smoke drift from his mouth without a breath to propel it. "You're a security guard watchin' over a deserted shithole inn in the dark of night. You're hardly livin' high on the hog." He raised his hands palm out. "Just sayin'."

"Hey Danny, what gives? He leavin' or stayin'?" someone called, and the man, Danny, looked at Pete expectantly.

Something to prove, Pete thought. *I'm always walking away. My son died and I walked away. They came to Claire's house and broke her window, almost broke us, and I walked away, and now, just when things were starting to look up, I'm getting ready to walk away again. It never stops.*

"Danny, what the fuck?"

"Shuddup a sec, willya? Guy's thinkin'."

Don't. A plea from the fractured, diluted image of Claire. *It'll work out in the end, Pete.*

But it never did. It never worked out, not the way he wanted it to, and now here was this stranger, a man in a suit that a hundred nights of watching over dead hotels would never pay for, offering him a chance to revisit the days when he'd known what magic was, when Lady Luck had been more than an interested glance from a beautiful woman. When he'd been a winner.

Slowly, he raised his head, unaware he'd been staring at the hammer, unsure why it suddenly seemed as if the sensible thing to do would be to bend down and retrieve it, and felt one last tug from behind him, urging him toward the front door and the cold night beyond. Where suddenly, without question, he knew nothing awaited him.

Danny's grin grew even wider. "You in?"

"Yeah, I'm in," Peter croaked, and inside the room where the laughing men were lounging and smoking cigars, another poker chip hit the pile. *Snick!*

* * *

Dawn. A pallid sun peered through a veil of cold rain as Gary Harrison turned his truck off Route 109 onto Stanton Street. He yawned and fingered the sleep from the corners of his eyes. Abigail Point was dead at this hour. Hell, during the off season it was dead at any hour, and the emptiness of it now, combined with the miserable weather, depressed him. It didn't help that he'd slept fitfully, most of the night spent wondering if hiring a one-time inveterate gambler had been a mistake that would end up costing him dearly. Sure the guy had claimed all of that was in the past, but during Gary's tenure as a cop, he'd spent enough time around chronic gamblers to know that the past was closer for them than it was for most people. But he'd also learned to read faces, and the desperation he'd seen in Haskins' eyes had seemed more like a genuine plea, a sincere need to find a way back into normal life, rather than mere jonesing for cash to blow on the tables. So, against his better judgment, and because he knew it was far from being in high demand, he'd given Haskins the Wickerwood job. But despite the confidence with which he'd sent the man on his way, the decision haunted him as soon as he laid his head down on the pillow at home. That Mike had made the miraculous and extremely rare decision to throw caution to the wind and spend the night with him, hadn't helped as much as he'd hoped. Their intimacy had been merely a distraction. Later, he'd envisioned all the possible repercussions that could result from hiring a man with Haskins' past. Over an early breakfast, he'd mentioned it to Mike, who of course was more preoccupied with the possible ramifications of his staying the night away from home, reminding him, for the umpteenth time, what would become of the town's squeaky clean image if the press got wind of their 'meetings'. All of which was preposterous, of course, and Gary told him so, adding that Abigail Point hadn't been 'squeaky clean' since the first settlers drove the

Tuckahoe Indians off their land to build the damn thing. As usual, that drew little more than a roll of the eyes and an exaggerated sigh from Mike, and there the discussion ended.

Communication, Gary feared, together with Mike's overblown perception of how important his job made him, was the straw that was eventually going to snap their camel's spine.

A faint rumble of thunder echoed in the distance as Gary aimed the truck down Jericho Street.

The inn, despite the beauty for which it had once been known, looked ugly in the feeble light of dawn, its dark facade like an ancient expression of scorn, reluctant to let go of the night and the cover darkness had provided it. Gary guided the truck to the curb, killed the engine, and stepped out into the street.

He looked at the inn. The inn looked back.

The thought that he'd made a big mistake, coupled with yet another morning greeted by Mike's stubborn refusal to accept the reality that no one in Abigail Point would give a rat's ass about his sexual preferences brought a sour feeling to Gary's gut.

Not to mention the inn, and whatever might await him inside.

It was going to be a bad day.

* * *

The heat was stifling. With a curse, Gary quickly crossed the lobby and switched off the construction heater. "I said in *intervals*, goddammit." His mood even darker than it had been before, he carefully negotiated a path around the toolboxes and machinery and stopped in the center of the room. "Hey Haskins," he called out. "You here?"

It was a silly question. The chains by the unlocked front door, the heat and the lights all told him that Haskins was here, unless the guy got spooked and left early, in which case the next order of business for Gary would be a good reaming of his former employee, if he had the restraint to leave it at that. Today was not the day to test his patience. "Hey," he roared. "Where you sleeping? C'mon, wakey, wakey!" His own voice rolled back to him in soft echoes. "Jesus." The majority of the stuff Securicorp had been hired to look after was in the lobby, so naturally that was where the man assigned to watch over them should be. But he wasn't, and that didn't bode well.

66

On the verge of letting out another cry, this one laden with all sorts of creative invectives, Gary spotted something gleaming dully on the carpet in the hall, a few feet past the door. Cry forgotten, he sighed and made his way over.

It was a hammer, he saw, and when he picked it up--for use as a weapon, just in case he had seriously underestimated Haskins' reasons for not responding--the handle was icy cold. He shivered, and shoved the tool, handle first, into his jeans pocket, so the head was still protruding and would be easy to grab if he needed it in a hurry. At six-foot one and two-hundred-and-forty pounds, he considered himself a match for any man in a fistfight, but was not naive enough to believe he could punch his way around a bullet.

"Haskins?"

Wood creaked somewhere above his head and he looked in that direction, as if he might be able to glean from the sounds some idea who had made them. "Hey, you there?"

No reply. The smell of dry rot and damp was near suffocating the further Gary moved down the hall, and he felt a pang of guilt that he hadn't equipped Haskins with a mask. For all he knew the guy was passed out somewhere with a lung full of spores.

Near the end of the hall, where single doors faced each other, the air grew denser still and Gary put a hand over his mouth. Another creak, louder than before, sounded from the room to his right, and he paused for a moment without being entirely sure why. He was reminded of a question he'd put to Haskins during the interview. While the other man stood before him dressed in a suit at least two sizes too big, Gary had sat forward in his comfortable leather office chair, a cup of coffee clamped between his large meaty hands, and asked, "Are you superstitious? Knock on wood and all that tripe? You believe in ghosts?" Haskins had said "no" and though Gary had simply nodded satisfactorily, he could have replied, "Good, glad to hear it. There's no way in hell *I'd* spend the night alone in that house," because he *was* superstitious, and he *did* believe in ghosts. As a kid, even when the inn had been alive and well and flourishing, it had made his flesh creep. He had heard some of the stories that didn't make the papers, had listened intently to the tales told by men his parents claimed were drunks and lunatics, and he hung on their every word, because his mind was wide open and willing to be populated with ghosts. He had *believed* with a fervor maturity didn't lessen and now, standing with a cold hammer stuck in his belt loop, in the damp moldy hallway of the very building that had given him nightmares and been the obvious focus of many a childish dare thirty years before, he was forced to recall that belief, because abruptly it seemed as if the building had grown heavy with expectancy, the silence strained and artificial, as it might if it was his birthday and all the guests were hiding, waiting to jump out and yell "Surprise!"

"Haskins?" He resolved that that would be his last time hailing the man. If Haskins wasn't here, then perhaps his absence represented a wise decision on his part, because Gary was starting to realize that thirty years of experience hadn't lessened the unpleasantness of the shadows inside the Wickerwood, the feeling of a thousand eyes studying you, the dusty, poisonous air that hung in every room like the memory of an argument.

He had to leave.

Before he did, guilt made him at least poke his head into the room to his right, and survey the area that had once been the lounge, frequented by rich drunks and richer gamblers. The bar and all the furniture had long since been removed, of course, which made it all the more unusual that an old green-felt poker table had been left sitting in the center of the room. It was surrounded by drop-cloths, plastic sheeting and the hunched, lopsided silhouettes of old beer crates, all of which were backlit by a halogen lamp positioned in the far corner, making them look like ghosts that had fallen asleep watching the gamblers. These specters of Gary's imagining were the only occupants in the room, and he turned, relieved—

BANG.

He froze, a startled cry lodged in his throat.

Then it happened again and he flinched, hard.

No subtle sounds were these; no vague structural protestation from a long abandoned house. This was a startlingly loud series of thumps against the floor, like a man with bowling balls for shoes hurrying to cross the room.

BANG.

BANG.

An involuntary gasp escaped Gary and he swiveled round, one hand dropping to the hammer, his mind already plotting the fastest route back to his truck, and when he saw there was still no one there, no hideous, rotten, undead thing hurrying to snatch him into its ethereal arms, no swiftly moving revenant clattering its chains against the floor, he felt no better.

BANG

BANG

BANG

Slowly but steadily making its way toward him from somewhere in the darkness beyond the poker table, bouncing with all the ease of a basketball in capable hands, was a bloodstained rock, hammering against the floor as if thrown in anger, then miraculously rising again into some unseen hand.

Faster and faster it rose and fell, each impact hard enough to leave craters in the wood.

BANG, BANG, BANG, *BANG*.

Closer and closer it came, but only when it was almost at the door where he stood paralyzed with terror, only when it was close enough for him to see the misspelled name of his former employee written in black marker across the bloody still-wet surface of that rock, and only when the slumbering plastic sheeting in the lounge suddenly wrenched itself upward with a deafening snap, did Gary run screaming from the inn.

SELDOM SEEN IN AUGUST

SELDOM SEEN IN AUGUST

Sirens wailed three blocks away.

Garden railings and high wooden fences whipped past Wade as he ran, his feet pumping the earth hard enough to send bone-jarring jolts through his legs. Frantic, he cast desperate glances at the houses whose backyards let out on either side of him. Each one seemed to be a carbon copy of the other, their windows visible over the fences like the eyes of mischievous children. They all appeared new too, which made sense to Wade. After all, he'd lived in this city his whole life, knew its highways and byways as if the veins on the back of his hand were a topographical map, and couldn't remember ever seeing a street called Seldom Seen Drive before. He figured it had materialized while he was in jail. Good thing he didn't give a shit about preserving Harperville's historical assets or he might have taken offense at the audacity of the city's planners, because if memory served, an old cathedral had once occupied the space where now stood about sixty cookie cutter homes. Whoever had purchased the lot had apparently done so without fear of divine retribution, and though Wade appreciated that kind of balls-to-the-wall confidence, he had no time to ponder it.

As he ran, the gaps between the fences made the neatly manicured lawns flicker like projections from a vintage show reel. Here and there he saw brightly colored toys scattered in the grass, or doghouses missing their dogs, the chains snaking into the grass and ending in nothing, as if the animals had burrowed down into the earth and died there.

Breath like fire in his lungs, he picked up the pace, sweat running freely down his back, dripping from beneath his arms, slithering into his eyes in an effort to blind him. The midday sun was a helicopter spotlight roasting the skin on the nape of his neck. In a body that felt like it was cresting a thousand degrees, the only cool spot was at the base of his spine, where his revolver was tucked snugly into the waistband of his jeans.

All the gates appeared to be locked, and all the locks looked the same. Wade wondered idly if the community had a pre-approved list of merchants they dealt with for such things, and thought he wouldn't survive a minute in such an anal-retentive neighborhood.

The alley between the rows of houses seemed endless, but the sirens kept him moving. Sooner or later it would open out onto a larger street—Kendrick Avenue, if he remembered correctly—and then he'd be even more exposed. And that was not good, not when the cops were so goddamn close. He had to find a place to hide, if only for a little while, just long enough for the cops to expand the radius of their search somewhere other than right up his ass.

He was thinking clearly and that was good, because the adrenaline was doing its best to disorientate him, making him feel as if he was a cartoon character, fleeing for miles past a looping, unchanging background.

Sirens wailed two blocks away.

Dammit. Rather than quicken his pace, he slowed to a jog. This was getting him nowhere, because although he had kept himself in shape over the years and could easily run for another ten miles if he had to, the reality of the situation was this: He was on foot, the cops were in cruisers. How long did he think it would take them to catch up? The only reason they hadn't already done so was because he suspected they weren't entirely sure where he'd gone, so for a brief time, the advantage had been his. But it wouldn't take much looking to spot him, thus, whatever he was going to do would have to be done fast.

You've got a gun, chief, he told himself. *Use it. You're surrounded by houses. Houses with* people *in them. People who have cars and can be* persuaded *to transfer ownership.*

The jog became a trot that became nothing. He stood still, the sirens sundering the hazy air around him. He had maybe five minutes before those cruisers came tearing through the alley. He looked at the nearest gate to his right. Locked, just like the others. It also seemed

that every single one of the gates had a BEWARE OF DOG placard
screwed onto it, as if having a mutt was a requirement of occupancy
here in Stepford. A moment of scanning, however, revealed a gate a
few houses down that didn't. Remembering the dog-less chains and
vacant kennels, he decided this was the safer bet. It wouldn't do to
break into a yard and get mauled, a possibility that might still be
realized if it turned out the sign had simply fallen down, or been
blown off. His options scarce, he decided to take the chance and
made his way toward it.

He wasn't surprised to see yet another padlock.

He reached for his gun then thought better of it. The sound of the
shot would be like a public announcement, and besides, shooting
locks only worked in the movies. In real life, chances were if the
bullet hit the hard steel casing, it would bounce right back and put a
hole in him. He thought about using the butt of the gun as a
hammer, but that didn't seem reasonable either. It would take too
long and his hands were so sweaty he didn't have much faith in his
ability to keep a hold on the barrel.

Wade put a hand to the wood, craned his neck to peer at the
width of the slats and nodded one time.

To hell with it. He positioned himself squarely before the gate, drew
back and delivered a solid kick to the panel just beneath the padlock.
The lock rattled, stayed intact, but the panel itself swung in from the
bottom like a cat-flap. Another kick to the adjacent panel and he had
a gap wide enough to squeeze through, which he did without pausing
to look for splinters or jagged spurs of wood that might cut his
throat. Once inside, he cast a quick look over the house for a sign
that his less-than-subtle entry had alerted someone, then, satisfied
that the eyes of the windows had developed no unwelcome pupils, he
quickly inspected the gate. The first panel was still attached, albeit
barely; the second had been blown out entirely. That wouldn't do.
Leaving it as it was would be as good as erecting for the cops a sign
with an arrow pointing toward the house. He made a hasty but
serviceable job of setting the panels so they appeared undamaged. Of
course, all it would take would be a nudge and the hole would reveal
itself, but with any luck he'd be long gone from here before anyone
thought to try. Plucking the largest of the splinters from the grass and
pocketing them, he moved fast and low toward the house, one hand
behind his back, fingers pressed against the butt of the gun.

A pair of garden gnomes, their bearded faces split wide by identical smiles, regarded him without judgment as he stepped onto the pristine patio and hurried into the cool shadow thrown like a dirty rug at the foot of the house. To his right was a koi pond, the colorful fish wavering lazily in an artificial current among polished stones made rough by algae. A stunted elm leaned over to gaze into the water. From one of its palsied branches hung a quartet of fake robins spinning in eternal circles, their route dictated by a motorized brass hoop. One of the robins was missing a leg, which Wade found oddly amusing despite the uncomfortable feeling of familiarity that came, he could only assume, from seeing so many bloody yards and their inane accoutrements.

He was startled then by the screech of tires and the staticky squawk of a radio from somewhere up the street.

Shit. They were almost on top of him, and he congratulated himself on having the sense to make the gate appear unbroken. With one hand still behind his back, he grabbed the gun, hefted it and hurried to the pair of sliding glass doors directly ahead of him. Only darkness showed within. Cupping his hands around his face he peered inside. He could just about make out the hunched silhouettes of furniture, the dull gleam of a mirror, but no movement, which didn't mean that someone wasn't in there, just that he stood a better chance of gaining access before anyone noticed.

Yeah, right.

There were any number of flaws in his plan, and though he tried not to think about them, they persisted, driven by self-preservation to remind him of the risk.

The door might be alarmed.

Someone might be waiting inside, hidden in the shadows with a gun aimed at where Wade now stood second guessing himself.

One of the neighbors might be watching him, a phone to their ear as they quickly related to the emergency operator what they had seen, and were seeing still.

Paranoia brought upon him the undeniable sensation of being watched. He felt it lying like a cape across his shoulders. The hair on the nape of his neck prickled and he glanced back over his shoulder. There were windows all around him, staring vapidly down from over a labyrinth of privacy fences.

He shook his head. Flaws, or not, he didn't have a choice. It was hide or keep running and he could only run so far before they wore him down. He reached out a hand, closed his eyes for a moment, and gripped the cold metal handle on the sliding door. *C'mon, you sonofabitch*, he thought, and pulled. To his amazement, the door slid open with a soft *whoosh*.

He paused on the threshold, listening, heart hammering against his ribs.

There was no sound from within.

Wade smiled. Another furtive glance over his shoulder, and he was inside.

* * *

The interior of the house offered no surprises.

Wade gently slid the door shut behind him and locked it, then pulled the curtains.

He turned to inspect his surroundings, but it was hard to make anything out in the gloom. What he could tell was that beneath his feet was a carpet that had seen better days and the air smelled faintly of furniture polish and pine air freshener. He did not need to know what the room looked like, only that he was the only one currently occupying it.

He felt a little better now that he was off the street and hidden, though he remained intrinsically aware that this did not constitute freedom. He was far from out of the woods. Anything could still go wrong, and in cases like this, usually did. Until he knew that he was alone in the house, he wouldn't let his guard down. Even then, he would remain on edge until a viable long-term escape plan presented itself, *if* one presented itself and he wasn't just dawdling here while a juggernaut of doom bore steadily down upon him.

Goddamn you anyway, Cartwright, he thought, clenching his teeth in frustration. He remained where he was, standing in the darkness by the drawn curtains, listening.

The house was quiet as the grave.

Not fool enough to take that as proof that he was alone, Wade cocked the gun as quietly as he could, which was not quiet at all, and slowly crossed the room, bound for the door in the wall opposite. Twice he barked his shin against furniture that had been lurking in the dark and had to restrain a gasp of pain. At length, ankle throbbing, he found the door and beside it a light switch he yearned to turn on, but resisted just in case it gave him away should someone be waiting for him in the hall.

Quietly, he opened the door.

A naked bulb cast sickly yellow light down on the narrow hallway.

There were coats, children's by the look of them, hooked over the newel post at the bottom of a short flight of carpeted stairs. A punctured football sat on one step beside the naked head and torso of a baby doll. Its eyes were closed as if sleeping. Wade gave it only the most cursory glance. He hated dolls, and had ever since that movie he'd seen as a kid in which one of them had opened its eyes in a darkened bedroom and grinned at a terrified child. The stupid movie hadn't even been about dolls, he recalled, and shook his head as he edged into the hall.

Ahead of him was a doorway, the light from the hall unable to reach very far over the threshold. *There's no one here*, Wade told himself. He was alone. He could feel it, but he knew better than to rely solely on instinct. Last time he'd trusted his gut, he'd enlisted Cartwright to help him with a heist and now six people were dead and the police were hunting them both. Unless of course they had already caught Cartwright, and Wade might not have been bothered to learn that was the case had his idiot partner not been lugging around with him the fifty grand or so they'd cleared from the bank job.

He moved on, back pressed to the wall, until he was inside the kitchen. It smelled like disinfectant in here, and he imagined the chaos of a busy family in the morning: kids yelling and shoveling cereal into their maws while their parents got dressed and tried not to let show the hatred and regret they felt for their own lives and each other. He pictured a woman, just this side of good-looking, her teeth grit as she vigorously scrubbed down the kitchen surfaces while pretending the sponge was a lathe and the counter her husband's face. They would exchange pleasant farewells for the sake of the kids, all the while secretly wishing fatal misfortune on one another.

Misery.

Wade had lived it, and so found it easy to envision. Indeed, though he recalled little of his childhood, so generic was this house that it summoned what unpleasant memories he had retained of it.

Pain.

Anger.

Annoyed, he shook off the reverie before it could properly take hold of him and moved further into the kitchen, sure now that he was alone in the house. The kitchen was empty. The dirty cups, bowls, and glasses piled in the sink in the center of the L-shaped counter confirmed his suspicion that what he had walked into was the aftermath of an ordinary morning in a hectic household. It was Monday; if he was lucky, the family would be gone until early evening when school and work relinquished its hold on them. If not, and someone came home for lunch, things could get ugly. He hoped it wouldn't come to that.

There was a small calendar tacked to a corkboard beside the refrigerator. He noted that today's date had been circled in red marker. August 16th. The picture above it was of a lush green meadow, speckled with dandelions beneath a sprawling blue sky. It might have been a pretty scene if not for the monstrous black satellite dish dominating the right side of the picture, the red tip of its phallic probe turned heavenward.

After uncocking the gun and tucking it back into his waistband, Wade opened the refrigerator and helped himself to some milk, straight from the carton. He belched and, still thirsty, exchanged the milk for a cold bottle of water, which did a better job of soothing his parched throat. His stomach growled, but he decided that could be dealt with after he'd inspected the upper rooms. He finished the bottle of water and tossed it in the trashcan, then moved to the large window, which looked out on the street. Cautiously, he fingered open the Venetian blinds.

Cars sat silently beside curbs.

Windows reflected the clear blue sky.

Sunlight through the sycamore trees painted leopard skin patterns on the sidewalks. Heat shimmered on the road.

But there was nobody on the street, no neighbors enjoying a day off, no retirees out mowing their lawns, no housewives gathering up the morning paper, no dogs barking despite the signs he'd seen that claimed the place was chock full of them. It was completely deserted, which was odd. If he'd chosen a dilapidated neighborhood as his hiding place, the absence of people would not have bothered him so much, but Seldom Seen Drive, while clearly not upper class, was no ghetto either. There should have been someone out there.

And you should be thankful that there isn't, he told himself and a moment later nodded his agreement. There would be countless obstacles in his path before he made it home free, he knew. Better not to question the things that weren't a problem.

He let the blinds snap back into place and returned to the hall. Averting his gaze, he stepped over the doll torso and quietly ascended the stairs. The further up he went, the darker it got until his progress slowed to a crawl and he was left fumbling for a light switch. Again he was reminded of the danger of switching on a light before he had explored the whole house, but concluded that it was equally dangerous to be trying to explore it blindly.

"Shit," he hissed, almost tripping when his foot connected with something hard and unyielding. He steadied himself, dropped to his haunches and listened for signs that someone had been drawn to his presence on the landing, but heard nothing. Only his own steady breathing. He squinted down at the floor and reached out with his hands until they touched on something smooth and round. An attempt to form a picture with his hands of what the object might be proved fruitless, so he lifted it, surprised by the weight, and lugged it over to the head of the stairs where he set it down on the top step.

It was a large pink ceramic pig with a slot in its back.

Jesus, Wade thought. *A friggin' piggy bank.*

It was loaded with coins, but why it had been left in the middle of the landing, like a lure for thieves pettier than he, was a mystery that immediately seemed less of one when he reminded himself that children lived here. Not without difficulty, he shoved it aside and thought that maybe he'd rob it after all, just because it had inconvenienced him. Besides, it would do the kid who owned it good to learn a hard lesson about life early on, so maybe the shit that lay ahead of them wouldn't be nearly so surprising.

He stood, turned, and flipped the switch on the wall behind him. The landing flooded with stark white light from another unshaded bulb and he raised a hand to shield his eyes. Spastic shadows slipped under the three doors on the second floor and down the stairs as he blinked ghostly orbs from his eyes.

Nice house like this, he thought. *No shades. Fucking weird.*

He took a step and put a hand on the nearest door. It swung easily open revealing a cramped, unremarkable bathroom that seemed unsuitable for anything but a bachelor who didn't mind getting piss in the sink. The shower curtain was spotted with mildew and pulled back to reveal a bathtub with a pink slip-proof mat, a drain clotted with long dark hairs, and a decidedly unhappy looking rubber duck. Time and multiple saturations had erased the pupil of one eye, leaving it with a cataract, while the other stared myopically upward as if questioning the injustice of it all. Wade grinned and turned away.

In the absence of any ambient sound, the sudden vibration against his right thigh made him jump and he scowled, embarrassed and glad as hell that no one had seen his reaction. From the pocket of his jeans he withdrew a slim silver cell phone. It hummed faintly as he checked the display.

"About goddamn time," he muttered, and though he wouldn't have admitted it under duress, he was relieved to see his partner's name on the phone's readout. It meant two things: Cartwright was alive, and he was loyal enough to keep in touch. The opposite in either case would have meant a whole lot of money lost to the wind.

Beneath Cartwright's name was a flashing envelope icon. It was not a call but a text message. One of the last things Wade had barked at Cartwright had been "no calls, you hear me? I don't want to be hiding up a goddamn tree and have the cops find me by following my *Mission Impossible* ring tone." And he was glad he'd imparted that little caveat, for while there were no cops breathing down his neck at the moment, he still didn't know for sure that there wasn't someone hiding in one of the other two rooms. Turning the phone off hadn't been an option either. He needed to regroup with Cartwright once the heat died down a little, and the sooner he knew the score, the better. *If I don't hear from you by sundown*, he'd told his partner, *I'm going to assume one of two scenarios: (a) you got caught, or (b) you got greedy and decided to split with the money. If the latter happens, I won't come after you, because I probably wouldn't know where to start looking. That's just me being honest. So you'll probably get away with it. I won't dog you. Instead I'll visit your family and you can see what I've done to them on the main evening news from whatever hole you're hiding in, got it?*

And apparently, Cartwright had.

Wade pressed the green phone symbol and the text message spread across the screen:

SRRY. FUCT UP

Wade bit down on his lower lip, his breath whistling through his nose. What the hell did that mean? *Sorry, I fucked up.* Was he referring to his little rampage at the bank despite Wade telling him only to shoot if someone got brave? Or was this some new turn of events? Had he lost the money?

Aggravated, he quickly hit REPLY and thumbed the buttons until he had typed:

FUCT UP HOW???

He hit SEND and cursed a little too loudly. He ran his free hand through his hair and caught a whiff of himself. The odor was rank, unpleasant, like sour cream, an unnecessary reminder that he needed to take a shower. And he would, but not here. He was relatively fearless, but not enough to totally disregard common sense by taking a soak in the house he'd broken into.

Agitated and eyeing the phone in the hope that he wouldn't have to wait long for the response, he pushed away from the wall. "C'mon, c'mon," he whispered urgently, willing Cartwright to respond. If it turned out the money was gone, Wade figured he might as well come out with his hands up. His share of the takings wouldn't be nearly enough to pay back the men who were out to break his legs, but it would keep them off his back for a while. Without it, he was as good as dead. And if they didn't get to him first, the cops surely would. But if he settled some of his debt, he still ended up with nothing, which was why Wade planned to kill Cartwright and take his share. It would be just enough to finance his relocation somewhere south of the border. It was a cliché, sure, but one that held endless appeal. He liked the sun, he liked Mexican food, and he liked dark women. Where was the catch?

So intent was he on the phone's display that it took him a moment longer than it should have to sense that there was someone standing behind him. Hair standing on end, body braced for the feel of slugs punching into his flesh, he turned, fumbled for the gun, but by the time he had it withdrawn, cocked and aimed at where the—*what?*—had been standing only a split-second before, it had vanished into the bathroom, slamming the door shut so hard behind it that for a moment Wade thought he'd pulled the trigger.

"Jesus H," Wade murmured, his heart thundering. For a moment he stood there, vacillating, unsure what to do next. Only when he carefully walked himself through what he'd just seen did he realize how convinced he'd been that there had been nobody in the house with him. And perhaps he hadn't been *entirely* wrong. After all, he couldn't be certain that whoever had scurried into the bathroom hadn't just come home. Wade hadn't heard a car, or a door, but that didn't mean squat.

No, he told himself. *No…they were here all along.*

His hackles rose, his senses on full alert now. He had let himself get complacent after the exhaustion of the chase, and that was an amateurish mistake to make, one that might have been his last.

Swallowing a lump the momentary shock had lodged in his throat, he pocketed his cell phone and took a step closer to the bathroom door.

It was a kid, he thought. *A teenager maybe.*

Not that it mattered a damn. He had no interest in taking hostages, only lives, especially those that intersected with his in ways in which he didn't approve.

Slowly, he dropped to one knee and brought his face close to the latch panel, his eye to the keyhole. He squinted, caught a glimpse of a bare chest rapidly rising and falling, the acne-flushed cusp of a chin. It was a boy, probably no more than fifteen or sixteen, sitting on the toilet, terrified.

Wade exhaled explosively, his knees cracking as he stood up.

"Hey," he said evenly. "Hey kid, come on out."

There was no answer, but he fancied he could now hear the faint hush-whisper of the boy's breathing as it quickened in panic.

"There's nowhere you can go. You understand that, right?" Wade said into the door. "You're stuck in there and I'm out here with a gun. What're your options?"

He waited a few moments, but the kid didn't answer.

"How about I give you three seconds to open the door, huh? One way or another, this hide-and-seek game's gonna end, but it'd be easier on us both if you just came on out of there on your own. One…"

Despite what many people had said over the past twenty years, Wade would get no pleasure at all from what he was about to do.

"Two…"

But that didn't alter the inescapable reality of the fact that it had to be done.

"Three."

* * *

Gun held low, he kicked in the door so hard the jamb splintered and sent daggers of wood flying. Bringing his weapon up to draw a bead on the kid sitting on the lid of the toilet, he expected screaming, crying, pleading. What he got was silence. The kid, pale and hollow-eyed and stripped to the waist, didn't even look at him. He just sat with his head down, looking at the straight razor he held in one hand, his chest rising and falling rapidly, the breath hissing in and out of his nose.

"Okay," Wade said. "Nice and easy now…"

In response, the kid made a strangled noise, then thrust his head back until it was resting against the wall and his green eyes were focused on the scabrous patches of mildew on the bathroom ceiling. His Adam's apple looked like a small fist pushing through white plastic as the kid stamped one bare foot against the floor and whined.

I know him, Wade thought, and felt his skin go cold.

It was a ridiculous notion and he shook his head to deny it. If the kid looked even remotely familiar it was because he lived in the same city. It was entirely likely Wade had seen him making his way to school one day, or hanging around outside one of the shadier clubs where grownups who had forsaken the thankless monotony of blue-collar life engaged in riskier but more lucrative pursuits. At such venues, Wade had once been a regular, and he'd often seen the children of gangsters hanging around outside, looking sullen that they'd been excluded from the proceedings, their eyes shining with ambition. A million years ago Wade himself had been one of them, had stood outside a warehouse that had appeared abandoned to anyone not affiliated with the people who owned it. But Wade knew what went on in there, and dreamed of the day he'd be enlisted to help one of the men on a job. That day had come, and it had helped to carve from shapeless useless clay the man he had become.

The kid began to weep.

Yes, Wade decided. *That's how I know him.* But he didn't believe a word of it.

"Listen," he said, "I want you to put that blade away, ok?"

The boy kept his head back, his eyes staring upward. Then he brought the ivory-handled razor up in front of his chest, the blade facing Wade.

Wade aimed for the head. "Put it away, kid. I'm not going to tell you again."

The blade hovered, reflecting both the harsh light and Wade's likeness back at him. He trembled for a moment in the boy's slender fingers. Then the razor carried on and up, stopping before his exposed throat.

"Hey…"

"*Sorry,*" the boy replied in the smallest of whispers, tears trickling down his gaunt face. The blade danced, and when the dance was over, there was a wide yawning smile just above his Adam's apple. Unlike Wade, the blood seemed almost hesitant to run.

"What the fuck?"

The boy continued to stare at the ceiling, at nothing. His hand fell away, the razor clattering off the bathtub, spattering the white surface with red periods before it hit the floor.

Wade let out a slow breath and lowered the gun. In some distant part of his brain, it registered that this development was a positive one—it had saved him an ugly job —but so unexpected and sudden had it been that he wasn't entirely sure how to react. Why had the kid killed himself? Because of him? As obvious a solution as that was, he didn't believe it. Over the years he'd become something of an expert in the human response to fear, to the threat he represented, and never before had he seen anything like this. Then there was the question of the straight razor. It hadn't been in the bathroom when Wade had checked it. He knew because it had been a nice one, and if it had been there, he'd have taken it as a souvenir, and possibly as an unpleasant *how-do-you-do* for the first cop who tried to cuff him. Of course, it could have been stashed in a drawer or something…

He ran a hand through his hair, scratched his eyebrow with the still cocked hammer of the gun and closed his eyes. A few moments of indecision later, he back stepped out of the bathroom and closed the door behind him.

You need to get out of here, he told himself.

As if the thought had been a cue, his cell phone buzzed. Glad of the distraction, he snatched it from his pocket. Cartwright again. Another text message. Wade hit the button. His partner's response was a single word, damning in its implications:

TALKED

So they'd caught him.

And the motherfucker had sung like a canary.

Wade felt such a surge of anger he grimaced in actual pain that burrowed up from his balls and twisted through him until it snagged in his throat and burst into flame. Face crimson, he started to tremble. A roar trapped behind his teeth, he aimed the gun at the floor, the walls, the closed doors at the end of the landing, his finger itching to squeeze off a few rounds to see if the clamor of the shots could compete with his own expression of rage.

"*Fuck!*" he yelled, for the moment uncaring about who did or didn't hear him. His muscles felt like ropes twisted to breaking, his blood like acid coursing through his veins. "*Goddamn* cock*sucker!*" Spittle flew from his lips as he spun on a heel back to the bathroom. In here was a piñata for all that violent anger, and hell, the kid wouldn't even mind, the little split-throat shit. He was beyond feeling anything anymore. But right now, Wade felt too much and he needed to hit something, needed to imagine the corpse in there had a different face, namely the pinched face of his backstabbing rat-bastard partner.

Cartwright, you're a dead man.

He shouldered open the door, a sneer on his lips.

The body was gone.

* * *

Phone in hand, Wade paced the landing. The sooner he was gone from this place the better, but every now and then he'd hear the distant squawk or the *whoop-whoop* of sirens as cruisers pulled to a halt, and it would remind him why he needed to be patient. Problem was, there was now a prankster running around out there covered in fake blood just dying to tell the cops about the guy he'd fooled. *Oh, and Officer, did I mention he broke in and had a gun?*

Wade cursed himself. What the hell was wrong with him? Had eleven years in the pen made him rusty or what? There was a time when he could have sniffed out a ruse without even being in the same building as the guy pulling it. But not only had he fallen for the kid's prank, he hadn't even realized the kid was in the house to begin with. He was getting old, that's what it was. Old and rusty, kept going by his addiction to vices and the consequential need to compensate for them with cash he didn't have. And that, he suspected, would never change.

"Hell with it," he said, and scrolled through the names in his cell phone's memory until he found one that read simply: "CUJ" which was an abbreviation for "Clean-Up Job", itself a code name for a man named Alex Eye, which no doubt was an alias but it was better than a series of stupid letters. Alex had proven useful, if ridiculously expensive, in the past when things hadn't exactly gone the way they'd been supposed to. Alex was six-foot six, black, and didn't speak a word. He just showed up, did what he'd been hired to do, then charged you up the ass and back down again for it. But he could untie the knot in almost any situation, thinking up clever escape plans where there didn't appear to be any. As a matter of pride, Wade had never used Alex's services. But he needed them now.

He made the call. Listened to the dial tone buzzing in his ear.

Paced.

Stopped when a phone in one of the rooms he was facing began to ring. He frowned, hung up on his call and cocked his head slightly.

The house phone stopped ringing.

He waited, expecting to hear whoever had answered muttering urgently inside the room. *Please help me there's somebody in my house!* But they were either being painfully quiet, or the person calling had given up. Wade waited a few more minutes. The doors to the rooms he had not yet investigated faced each other across the narrow landing. He hit the SEND button on Alex's number, and walked slowly to the door on the left.

The call went through.

Inside the room on the right, the house phone began to ring again.

"What the hell is going on?" he mumbled, and took the phone from his ear to check the display. Alex's name showed above the miniature icon of a phone ringing so violently the receiver was dancing. Frowning, Wade jabbed the END button, canceling the call, and immediately raised his eyes to the door from which the ringing sound had come.

It stopped.

He surprised himself by chuckling and shaking his head, as if he'd just been told a hoary old joke but owed it to the teller to laugh.

"I'll be damned," he said. "Now *that's* clever."

Just to be absolutely sure, he tried Alex's number again.

The house phone rang.

Hung up.

The phone went quiet.

A single bark of laughter and he pocketed the phone, raised the gun. "Jesus, I never..." he said, wiping a tear from his eye. "But...*how?*"

A number of possible explanations came to him.

One: By some miracle or coincidence, he had broken into Alex's home, which would explain why the house phone was ringing when he dialed the man's number.

Wade groaned.

Two: Alex had some kind of weird but ingenious redirect function attached to his number that, rather than lead to an answering machine, led to the phone nearest the caller.

Wade closed his eyes.

Three: Someone was fucking with him.

Wade opened his eyes.

Enough.

In three short steps he was at the door on the right and throwing it wide. It thumped against the far wall and shuddered back toward him, giving him the deeply unpleasant sensation that the room was shrinking while he watched.

The sunlight stretched languidly into the room through net-curtained windows, spotlighting the fall of dust motes to the bare wood floor. An old vanity squatted in shadow in one corner. In another was a rocking chair. Atop it sat an old black rotary phone. In the center of the room was a bed with a single dirty white sheet, and beneath it lay a woman, her long silver-gray hair spread out around the stained pillow.

Wade put a hand out to stop the door from closing, and stepped into the room.

The old woman shifted, turned her head. "Billy?"

Her voice, like the room, was dusty.

"'Fraid not," Wade said. "And who might you be?"

The old woman rose out of the bed like a specter. There was no series of movements, just one fluid one, as if she were attached to ropes threaded through hooks in the ceiling. One moment she was on her back, an ordinary old lady, the next she was floating toward him like something out of a horror movie, her feet tangling in the sheets, pulling them away, revealing the bloodstains on the mattress beneath.

Gooseflesh rippling all over him, Wade retreated from the room, his attempt to shut the door behind him so frantic he missed the knob on the first try and had to lean in to make a second one.

The lady, in no hurry at all, drifted toward him and now he could see that she was blind, that her teeth were gone, that her flimsy nightdress was spattered with blood both old and new.

She was almost upon him, her withered arms outstretched toward him in a gesture of pleading or longing, her face twisted into an expression of such profound sadness it almost drained the energy from him.

"Jesus," he said and pulled the door shut, but not before he heard her say, "You never come to see me anymore, Billy…"

He stood there, perplexed and unsettled. Just what in the blue hell was going on? Had he broken into a lunatic asylum masquerading as a suburban home?

As he stood there, his brain telling him that the best course of action, the *only* course of action now was to get moving, get as far away from this madhouse as possible, he heard a humming sound he at first assumed was his phone. *Cartwright*, he thought with a by now familiar flare of anger, but the cell's display was dark, the phone quiet. The humming was coming from the walls.

"Okay," he muttered. "Okay, we're done."

He turned, intending to head back across the landing, down the stairs, and out, when the door to his left, the only one he hadn't yet opened, creaked and swung wide, exposing the room beyond.

Go, Wade told himself, absently slipping the cell phone back into his pocket. *Don't bother looking in there. Just go.*

But without being fully aware that he was doing so, he moved slowly to the door and peeked inside.

The floors and walls were blackened, as if by fire. The air smelled like soot and charcoal, and burnt meat.

The windows were boarded over.

There was no furniture.

Staggering drunkenly toward him was a woman with a broken neck. She was naked, her heavily veined breasts like punctured balloons hanging down over ribs that poked through her mottled blue skin. One broken-fingered hand covered the dark thatch of her pubic hair in a gruesome parody of modesty. Her head had been twisted almost all the way around, the skin on her neck bunched into folds. He could see the ridge of one ear, the faintest curve of a bloody smile as she tottered like an infant toward where he stood, horrified. There were needle marks on her arms and legs and feet, and he could not stop looking at them.

The woman gargled, then flickered.

Wade blinked rapidly.

The woman flickered again, like a movie with gaps in the reel, like the yards seen through the fences as he'd fled, and then she changed, whined much like the boy in the bathroom had. Abruptly the film jumped and she became a terrible charred thing, patches of red visible through a veritable carapace of roasted flesh.

She stopped her tottering advance and screamed, and though it made little sense to him, it was that scream rather than the pantomime of broken-necked burning that made him remember who she was.

"Gail?" he said, and the door slammed shut so suddenly and so forcefully it cracked the wood and shattered the frame. Wade cried out in surprise, his attempt to back away foiled by something that had insinuated its way between his feet. The doll torso, he saw but was already falling, the notion of another cry dissuaded by the floor as his back thumped against it, winding him.

Though the instinct to flee was overwhelming, he stayed on the floor for a moment, eyes closed while he regulated his breathing.

So how do you explain this? he asked himself. *Did I break into a haunted house or what?*

No, he thought. *I didn't. It's a trick, and a damn good one, but a trick just the same.*

He slowly, painfully got to his feet.

Wade didn't believe in ghosts. In his line of work, he couldn't afford to. Bad enough that he spent his life looking over his shoulder looking for living enemies than have to consider the ones he'd already put in the ground. But it was clear that whoever had engineered this little theater production knew him, and had somehow managed to corral him here for a little show-and-tell. But to what end? And exactly how had they known he'd be *here*, in *this* particular house? Were all the others similarly booby-trapped? He might have thought that stoolie son of a bitch Cartwright had included Wade's hiding place among the notes he'd sung to the police, but Cartwright didn't *know* where he had gone after they'd split up.

That's when he thought of the gate.

The only one without a sign. And while Wade had no particular feelings about dogs one way or another, common sense dictated that a man seeking a haven would choose the path of least resistance. No psychological profiling necessary to glean that particular nugget. But what if he hadn't? What if, instead of choosing Seldom Seen as his hiding place, he'd run on and sought sanctuary elsewhere? He had *chosen* to come here, to *this* house in *this* neighborhood. Why then did he feel as if he'd been lured here?

No, it didn't add up. Factor free will into the equation and nobody could have known he'd have chosen this house, dog sign or no.

And yet, here you are.

Because of a sign, or rather, the lack of one?

The sign, he realized, and the sirens. He now recalled that those wailing sirens had seemed to come from everywhere, from all around him until he hit Seldom Seen Drive. Then they'd only been behind him. Closer and closer all the time until he felt trapped, vulnerable, desperate…

"Jesus, this is ridiculous," he said aloud and brushed himself off. He took a deep breath and slowly released it.

How are they doing this?

He didn't know, nor did he care. It was time to go.

A kick sent the doll torso flying over the balcony and down the steps. Wade listened to it tumbling, waited until it stopped, then followed it down.

* * *

At the foot of the stairs, he stepped on the doll and gave a start when it emitted the sound of a woman quietly sobbing. He had no wish to give this further consideration and so stalked through the house until he had reached the living room and the sliding doors he had used to gain entry.

Wade was no idiot. He knew that walking out there with the cops on his tail was likely to be the last thing he ever did, at least as a free man. But he couldn't stay here either. Not while there was someone hiding in the house who knew him, knew what he was and what he had done, someone who was having just the grandest time tormenting him with sideshow trickery. It all felt a little bit too predestined for his taste.

No. He was going, and he would just have to be careful once he crossed the threshold. He did not want to think about Cartwright and the money, and what it meant for his chances of a future. All that mattered now was getting gone.

Resolute, he stayed down and moved in a crouch to the curtains, parted them with a finger and felt his breath catch in his throat.

There were two cops in the yard, and they were heading toward the house, guns drawn.

"Great." Wade backtracked to the hall, then hurried into the kitchen where he flexed the fingers of his free hand, the sweat oozing from his pores, and tried to think. In seconds the cops would knock on the sliding door. After seeing the gate they wouldn't be so easily persuaded that nothing was amiss. They would force the door and they'd have him.

Keep it together, man, he told himself. *You've still got a weapon. You're not done, yet.*

But despite his own encouragement, he *felt* done.

Cartwright was gone.

The money was gone.

The pigs were at the back door and his hidey-hole was filled with spiders.

Check the front.

The rapping of hard knuckles against solid glass echoed through the house, each knock sending a jolt of electric fear up his spine.

Wade ran to the kitchen window, looked outside.

Two cruisers were parked at the curb, lights flashing. The trio of cops standing around them was the only sign of life on an uncannily empty street. If the sight of police hadn't lured the curious out of their homes, then it was quite possible that nobody lived in them after all. It put him in mind of the fake homes filled with mannequins the military set up in the desert as targets for nuclear testing.

His head hurt. Things had gotten way more complicated than they should have been. Rob the bank, nobody gets hurt, split up and meet later to divvy up the score. That was it. A simple plan. Instead, people had died, victims of Cartwright's itchy trigger finger, Wade was stuck in some kind of sick-joke carnival funhouse designed from blueprints straight out of his head, and now Cartwright was in custody and telling the cops...

Still looking out onto the street, he frowned.

Just what did Cartwright *have* to tell them? That he hadn't robbed the bank by himself? There were ample witnesses who'd testify to that, and if not, there were the security cameras. There wasn't much else he could give the pigs that they could use. Cartwright didn't know him well enough. He wouldn't, for instance, be able to tell them where he was likely to hide, or whom he might seek sanctuary from. In fact, Cartwright didn't know jack. So, assuming Wade had properly understood the text message, what exactly had he "TALKED" about? Who exactly had he "TALKED" to?

Then it clicked.

Not the cops, but the instigator of this little ghost house tour that had been set up in his honor. Whoever the Wizard behind the curtain was, he would need to know everything about Wade to be able to pull this off and had, it seemed, enlisted Cartwright's help in constructing the charade. Which in turn explained why the only "ghosts" Wade had seen had been ones he had managed to forget over the years. The minor transgressions. The puppet master of the house hadn't had access to his deeper, darker secrets or the show might have been an altogether more gruesome one.

He smiled. *Figured you out, you fuck.*

Glass shattered in the kitchen.

"Wade Crawford," one of the cops called. "This is the police."

You don't say, Wade thought and crossed the room, shoving his back up against the wall beside the kitchen door.

His phone hummed.

Christ, now what?

"Wade, we'd like to do this quietly if at all possible. We don't want anyone to get hurt, and that includes you. We just want to talk."

Wade hadn't fired a shot since he'd arrived at the house, out of fear that it would alert the cops to his position, but that was hardly a concern now. Fortunately, it meant he had a full clip now together with the extra one in his jeans pocket. He could hold them off for a little while, at least until a better option presented itself.

He took out his phone, slid his back down the wall until he was sitting, and peeked around the corner. There was nobody creeping up on him, but it wouldn't be too long before they would, right before the SWAT team arrived to teargas his ass. He checked the phone. Another message from Cartwright, and just as cryptic as before:

BSMENT

He studied the message for a brief moment before pocketing the phone. He didn't know if there was a basement in the house or not, and didn't much care. Basements were not traditionally famed for being good escape routes unless they had a series of intricate tunnels leading elsewhere. They were traps. And even if he'd chosen to overlook that glaring fact, he wasn't about to take advice from Cartwright now that he knew he was in on the whole thing.

So no, to hell with the basement.

An attic on the other hand...

It would still be trapping himself, but better the high ground than the low, and it would be difficult for anyone to get at him without getting a bullet to the head.

He almost laughed at the image of himself, knees drawn up, shooting a succession of cops one after the other as they poked their heads up into his hideout. It wouldn't work. The only option then was to shoot his way out and hope for the best.

Movement in the hall made his shoulders tighten. He leaned out and saw a young, fresh-faced cop doing the same thing. Only the cop looked surprised.

Even more so when Wade shot him in the head.

The cop fell back against the wall.

There was stunned silence for a second.

Then all hell broke loose.

More glass shattered, men shouted commands, furniture was overturned, more crashing, hammers were ratcheted back, static exploded from radios.

Wade grinned. "Get the message, you assholes?" he called out.

"You're a fucking dead man," one of the cops shouted back and was quietly reprimanded by another.

From one of the upstairs rooms came the sound of footsteps. They were penning him in, as if he wasn't already penned in enough.

As he prepared to rise into a crouch and make a break for the stairs, his plan to intercept whoever this latest unwelcome visitor was before the option was taken away, he noted that the doll torso had somehow found its way into the kitchen. It lay between his legs, eyes open and staring at him.

He rose onto his haunches.

"You hear me, Crawford?" the angry cop yelled at him, his voice cracking. "You're not walking out of here."

It was clear the young cop's death had hit the guy hard. *Boo-hoo,* Wade thought.

"What? You mean like that kid out there missing the top half of his head? Like him, you mean?" he called back.

The humming sound came again.

A quick check told him it was not his phone.

He tried to filter out the clamor from the cops as they tried to talk some sense into their incensed comrade.

Hunkered shadows moved past the kitchen window.

Shit.

He put a hand on the floor to steady himself, his mind buzzing.

Gotta be a way—

His fingers brushed against the doll and he recoiled. Was it his imagination or had the doll appeared to be shivering when he'd touched it? He returned its unwavering stare for a moment, until he realized he'd found the source of the humming sound.

The doll was vibrating.

Gunfire made him duck as a chunk of plaster and wood the size of a fist exploded from the doorway mere inches above his head. Gray dust rained down on his shoulders.

"Hear me now, you prick?" the cop roared at him.

Rustling in the hall again. Most likely the cop, whose movement the gunshot had been meant to cover, he assumed.

Well, this is it, he thought with curious calm, and took a deep breath, bracing himself to swing out around the kitchen door and plug another dumb cop. He cast one last look down at the doll and smirked.

The doll smirked back.

Wade flinched.

The doll opened its Cupid's bow mouth wide. Wider. Something glinted inside, and despite the horror, despite the urgency of the situation in which he was currently mired, Wade leaned forward and peered into that open plastic maw.

The doll began to hum again.

Needles, Wade realized, *it's got needles in its mouth*, and jerked back a second too late to avoid their trajectory as the doll winked and spat them into his face.

* * *

He awoke what felt like only seconds later, but clearly it had been more than that because he was no longer in the house, or at least in any part of it that he had seen during his turbulent time there. As the effects of whatever drug the needles had contained gradually abated, he was left with only a mild headache, slightly muddled vision, and a great disappointment not only that he had been caught, but also that he hadn't managed to take down a few more of the cops before the end. Not that he blamed himself for that. Who knew a doll could spit poison darts? He shook his head and it hurt.

They had bound him to a chair by his feet and ankles. In true modern fashion, they hadn't used ropes, but PlastiCuffs, the kind that you had to gnaw through your own limbs to escape. As expected, when he tested their hold, there was no give at all. He was, as Shakespeare had once said, well and truly fucked.

There was little to see in the room but a small blue card table, the cheap kind you could pick up at any convenience store. A chair was set on the other side of it. Behind the chair was a wall of television screens. The screens were on, but showed nothing but gray.

Wade waited.

At length a door opened somewhere behind him. He tried to see who was there but gave up when it caused fiery threads of pain to scurry up the back of his neck.

"Mr. Crawford?" the visitor asked in an oddly benevolent voice, as if he had been dying to make Wade's acquaintance.

"Yeah? Who're you?"

The man came around the table, allowing Wade to get a good look at him.

"My name is Hank Cochran. You may have heard of me?"

"Nope," said Wade.

"Ah. Well, no matter. We have plenty of time to get to know one another."

Cochran was silver-haired and dressed in a charcoal colored suit and a midnight blue tie. A matching handkerchief poked like the tongue of a hanged man from his breast pocket. As he sat and put his hands together, Wade saw that his nails were neatly clipped. The man's face was long and pale. Bushy eyebrows fought to unite over a pair of light blue eyes. Everything about him spoke of money, of a no-nonsense attitude toward life.

Wade wondered if he was a lawyer, a mortician, or a mobster. He looked like a combination of all three. Of course, many of the lawyers he'd known who'd worked for the mob had been forced to adopt all of those roles at one time or another. One thing he did know for sure was that the old man in front of him was not on the right side of the law.

"I'm sorry for keeping you waiting."

"No problem. It was a good chance to gather my thoughts."

Cochran looked at him, a faint smile on his face. "Do you know where you are, Wade? May I call you Wade?"

Wade shrugged. "So where am I?"

"Still in Seldom Seen."

Wade looked around again, noted the dirt walls around the bank of television screens, and nodded. "The basement, right?"

Cochran smiled, exposing brilliant white teeth. "Right."

"Why?"

"We're conducting a project here."

"And it's not arts and crafts."

"No. No it isn't. It's a little more elaborate than that, though I suppose there are similarities. Both require the coming together of certain elements to work."

"And I'm an element."

"You are, yes. A vital one." Cochran seemed to be enjoying their exchange, which baffled Wade somewhat.

"So what does the project entail?"

"Rehabilitation."

"By what means?"

Cochran raised his eyebrows. "Oh, but you've already seen the means." He looked up at the ceiling, which consisted of a network of wires and rotting beams Wade didn't think would take much to bring down. "Upstairs."

"The ghosts?"

The old man shook his head. "They're not ghosts."

"Holograms then."

"In a way, if you think of yourself as the projector."

"So you put on this show of things from my past in the hope that I would—what? Drop to my knees and pray for forgiveness?"

Cochran sat back and folded his arms. "That's the gist of it, though given your history, we'd all have been rather astounded if your reaction had been so dramatic, or so easily attained."

"What were you hoping for then?"

"Gradual dawning."

Wade pondered this a moment, then said, "Well if by "dawning" you mean figuring out your game, then I won, didn't I? What's my prize? Few hookers and some Cuban cigars? One-way trip to Mexico?" He grinned, but let it fade when he realized it wasn't being returned. Cochran suddenly looked all business.

"Wade," he said, leaning forward again, his palms flat on the table. "You're a psychopath."

"That's kinda strong, isn't it?"

"It's fact."

"Well, so's the fact that you're an old fart, but you don't hear me pointing it out."

"You killed a man three weeks shy of your fifteenth birthday. There was a boy with you. Do you remember?"

Wade remembered the man clearly, the boy only vaguely.

"Not the kid. Only met him that one time," he said. "But the guy had it coming."

"Or so you were told. That he deserved to die. If they'd said the same about anyone, whether it was true or not, you'd have done what they asked of you, wouldn't you?"

"I suppose so," Wade said. "It was the way things were."

"And it was the way you wanted it to be."

Wade frowned. "Have we entered the psychological evaluation stage of our relationship, Mr. Cochran?"

Cochran ignored him. "The boy's name was Eddie Scarsdale. Like you, he wanted to be a gangster, wanted some way to make a lot of money so he wouldn't get mocked at school anymore for having holes in the soles of his shoes, but he didn't have the *chutzpah*, the nerve to take the life of another human being. After you killed the old man, he was so distraught, so guilty, he went home and got his father's straight razor..." He waved a hand in the air. "You know the rest."

Wade thought of the kid in the bathroom upstairs and shook his head. "So it's *my* fault he took the chickenshit expressway?"

Cochran just stared, his face unreadable.

"Whatever," Wade said. "So who was the old floating bitch in the bedroom?"

"My wife," Cochran said evenly.

"Whoops." Wade chuckled. "I'd put my foot in my mouth if it wasn't tied to the chair."

"She was never the same after Eddie's death."

Despite the lingering skeins of disorientation, Wade was able to connect the dots fairly quickly. "Your wife?"

Cochran nodded.

"So then, this Eddie character was your son?"

"No."

"All right then, I'm lost."

"He was already dead by the time I met and married his mother."

"Gotcha."

"But I saw how she suffered. Saw how it ate away at her worse than any cancer." A distant look entered his eyes. "I think she married me just so she wouldn't be alone. Not sure there was any love there. At least, from her."

Wade leaned forward as much as his restraints would allow. "Can I interrupt you for a sec?"

Cochran waited.

"Thanks. Um...how did you get the impression from my record, which I assume you've read in detail, that I would give a cartwheeling fuck about anything you've just told me?"

Cochran shook his head.

"Hey, look, I am sorry about what happened to your...whatever he was to you, and your wife. Really, I am."

Cochran gave a feeble smile. "Perhaps you should care, Wade. It is, after all, part of the reason you're here."

"Okay, so what's the other part of the reason?"

"Do you know what nanotechnology is?"

"Computer classes for grandmothers?"

"Funny," the old man said. "But no, it refers to control of matter on the atomic and molecular scale."

"Sounds fascinating. And is it safe to assume that it also means we've moved from psychoanalysis to psychics? Because if we have, I'd like to apologize in advance if I nod off during your lecture."

"In this case, they're interlinked."

"You're losing me again."

"Then I'll condense it for you," Cochran said patiently. "In 2000, my company announced a breakthrough in psychotherapy following a fusion of two distinct but radically different departments of the University of Ca—"

"Jesus Christ, get to the point already," Wade said around an exaggerated yawn.

"Very well. What we developed was called "nanoreality"—a means of using nanotechnology to construct realistic visual images, or as you so rightly guessed, "mental holograms" based on the memories of a subject."

"Interesting," Wade said, sounding bored. "But it makes me wonder why you felt the need to strap me to a chair when just listening to you would have been enough to bore me into a coma."

Cochran continued, unfazed. "It was primarily developed as a way for doctors to abandon professional speculation and actually *see* the trauma in the minds of their patients, as if it were a movie, to witness firsthand the core of the patient's illness in living color, and therefore treat the patient accordingly. Of course the possibilities didn't end there. Witnesses afraid to talk, or abuse cases with repressed memories...all of it could be found in the subconscious and projected for observation and study. We could, in essence, see reflections gleaned from the subject's life. Better yet, a dying man could project images of his killer and we could save them. Better than any mugshot. It stands to turn the justice system as we know it on its ear."

Wade felt the restraints biting into his wrists. There was a way out of these zip-ties. Someone had told him how to do it once upon a time, but the method eluded him now.

"But like any great discovery, "nanoreality" had its problems, and some pretty significant ones at that. Once access was gained, we found it difficult to isolate the memories we wanted. The mind doesn't have an index, you see. It's like a library full of books with no titles. We ended up selecting them at random." He shook his head. "Which had unfortunate consequences for some of the subjects, otherwise good people who had seen terrible things and had managed to forget them. Essentially we made them relive those nightmares, and of course, when memories are recreated in front of you, they cease to be memories anymore. They become the present, the now. So those who had witnessed or endured tragedies were forced to witness them again. And once the present became the past again, the memory was duplicated, intensifying the level of emotional turmoil. It proved counterproductive, exacerbating the very symptoms we were trying to cure."

Wade smiled. "So you fucked them up even more, in other words."

"Yes," Cochran conceded. "And I'll spare you the speech about every great advance needing sacrifice. It was my fault. We weren't ready."

"But now you are?"

Cochran sat back again and appraised Wade for a long moment. Then he offered him a tight smile. "Yes. Many lives have been lost trying to perfect this thing. The initial project was deemed a failure and shut down until I decided to fund a new version of it. As you might imagine, the old concerns were revived right along with it, but I had done my homework this time. We had planned to go public until someone in my staff leaked word of the project to the press. It was not received well. They accused us of trying to steal the last of mankind's secrets, invading the only place left the government hadn't already probed. During this wave of negativity, the government men showed up, stirred from their nest by the media and on the warpath. After an admittedly impressive demonstration, I was able to keep them from shutting us down, but only if I agreed to sign the whole thing over to them when complete, with my role reduced to advisor."

"That had to suck," Wade said, grinning.

"Not nearly as much as I thought. You see, the advances we made in that three year period were phenomenal. We broke barriers we never imagined we'd break, and extended the realm of possibility almost infinitely. There is very little we can't do with this technology, but of course claims are nothing without proof." He smiled and joined his hands. "Which is where you come in."

Wade nodded his understanding. "I'm the guinea pig."

"Yes."

* * *

Wade was sweating again, but this time he was glad of it. Enough lubrication and he stood a better chance of slipping free of his restraints. Not a much better chance, but anything was better than nothing. And if he got free, the first order of business would be to strangle the boring old bastard with his own tie. He could think about what to do with the cops upstairs—assuming they were still there—later.

"So what's next?" he asked Cochran.

"We've already run through the first stage. Exposure to select memories to gauge your reaction."

"Which was disappointing if the reviews are to be believed."

"Yes, but as I said, hardly surprising."

A thought occurred to him then. "You said you weren't able to isolate individual memories, didn't you?"

Cochran seemed pleased. "So you were listening after all?"

"Can't help it," Wade said. "My ears don't listen to reason."

"Well, you're correct. We *weren't* able to isolate individual memories. But we figured it out. Now, not only can we pick and choose the memory, we can *transfer* them."

"What does that mean?"

"It means," Cochran told him, "that the memories you experienced upstairs didn't significantly affect you for a good reason."

"Which is?"

"Not all of them were yours."

"Hardly a shock," Wade said. "I wasn't there to see the kid die. I've never even seen the old w...your wife before. And..."

"Correct, but the last one, the hooker, couldn't have come from anybody's brain but yours."

For the first time since meeting the old man, Wade felt a pinch of anger in his belly. There was no denying that Gail, a girl he had loved, if only for a short time, had been a prostitute. God knows she'd turned him away enough times or asked him to wait in the diner downstairs because she was "entertaining" but then as now, he hated hearing her called a 'hooker'. It was, he knew, the typical reaction of the blind, those people who judged her based on how she looked and what she did rather than who she was. And if they'd known, they might have been surprised to find that she had a college degree (though in what, he no longer recalled), and a six-year old child she'd adored (but who lived with her mother for obvious reasons), and that she'd played piano like a virtuoso. She hooked to make enough money to buy a house for herself and her son, and she'd been pretty close to realizing that goal when she'd decided she'd had enough of Wade. A violent man by nature, he nevertheless managed to rein in his temper for her. Hurting her wasn't the way to secure her love, to persuade her that her life would be better with him in it, even if it only served as a constant reminder of what she'd done in the years before she made a clean break. So instead of beating her, he'd introduced her to drugs, and that had worked like a charm. She'd grown to depend on him again, to appreciate him, and that had lasted until the night she threatened him with his own gun. By that time, the drugs had completely taken hold of her, leaving her delusional, unreachable. When she'd pleaded with him to let her go, he knew she was talking to the cocaine in her system, in her brain, so that when he killed her, it was a mercy.

"Did I strike a nerve at last?" Cochran asked.

"Nope."

"Ah well," Cochran said, sounding not at all disappointed, "there's plenty of time."

Wade sighed. "Okay, let's quit fucking around. What am I doing here?" As he spoke, he tugged his arm up as much as the restraint would allow. The zip tie caught on his wrist-bone and moved no further. It would though, he was sure of it.

Cochran smiled broadly and gestured at the room around them. "It's actually quite clever. I shifted the focus of the project as needed to keep its validity in the eyes of those who might be swayed to pull the plug."

Wade closed his eyes, exasperated. "Good for you."

"I proposed, instead of concentrating solely on mental patients, that we expand our scope to include violent criminals. Not that I believe there's much of a difference, mind you. I suggested we build a fully functional neighborhood right in the middle of Harperville's black zone, where recidivism is out of control."

"Black zone?"

"The area worst affected by crime."

"Careful Reverend Sharpton doesn't get wind of that."

"It was to be, what my workers affectionately called a 'glue trap'. The objective would be to lure or force pre-selected criminals into the house chosen for them."

"Where they would be visited by the ghosts of Christmas past," Wade said with a smirk.

"In a sense, yes. Each house contains two-dozen hosts, which are units installed in the walls behind perforated plaster. When triggered—remotely, of course—they send out spores, nanobots, which are then inhaled. Once inside you, they begin to acquire your information, much like a system search on a hard drive. When they find what they want, they shoot signals against your eyes like a cathode ray will shoot electrons against a television screen. So what you're seeing in front of you, isn't really there."

"But why images that weren't mine?"

Cochran's smile disappeared. "A personal touch. A signature. For that, I'm sorry. It's not something I'm permitted to do, but I wanted you to see them. You've gone so long not feeling a damn thing for the lives you've destroyed. You killed a man. A child killed himself over it, and his mother went mad. I married her and watched it happen. And I didn't help. Didn't know how. Instead I buried myself in my work. Dedicated myself to finding a way to make remorseless killers regret what they did, and experience in vivid detail the pain they'd caused."

"Doesn't seem to have worked though, does it?"

"We're not finished, Wade." Cochran tilted his head and spoke in a low voice to someone who wasn't there. "Monitors, please."

Immediately the bank of screens behind him came to life. Each one showed a different man, and in one case a woman, exploring rooms similar to those in the house above Wade's head. Some of them had weapons, others looked as if they were the weapon.

"Who are they?" Wade asked, but already knew the answer.

"Criminals, just like you," Cochran said, without looking at the screens. "Murderers, rapists, drug-dealers, arsonists..."

"And you think the glue trap is going to work on them?"

"That's the hope, yes."

"Rats in a cage," Wade said bitterly. "To me it doesn't look like you've come that far from sixth grade biology." He watched as, on one of the screens, an enormous man riddled with tattoos, bent down to inspect something on the stairs in front of him. It looked like a jack-in-the-box.

"Perhaps," Cochran replied. "Or perhaps the key to our worst fears can be found in childhood games."

Wade thought of something and studied the television screens for a moment before he brought it up. "Where's Cartwright?"

"Hmm?" Cochran said, the faintest hint of a smile on his lips. "Oh, Cartwright, yes. He's not currently active."

"Active? You killed him?"

"I didn't, no. And the intent was never to take his life, but it would appear we still have a few bugs in our system."

"Huh."

"Does that surprise you?"

Wade nodded. "A little. You talk about this project of yours like it's going to be the greatest gift to mankind, but don't blink when you talk about someone dying because of it."

"It would be hard to defend my position without sounding like a Bond villain, Wade. Or worse, making me sound like you."

"Why stop now? I was enjoying the monologue."

"I'm sure, but I'm afraid you're not the only subject I have to deal with today." He half-turned and indicated the monitors with a sweep of his hand. On one of them, Wade saw that the woman was fishing through the kitchen drawer. She stopped and withdrew a long carving knife, then smiled.

"There's something I don't get," Wade said.

"Yes?"

"What was with the text messages?"

"How do you mean?" The sparkle in the old man's eyes suggested he already knew exactly what it meant.

"Who sent them?"

"Why, Cartwright, of course."

"What did they mean? That he'd talked to you?"

Cochran nodded. "Yes. Unfortunately, he was not as inclined as you were to follow the predetermined path. He strayed, so we had to rely on backup to bring him in. From the outset he knew the house was a ploy of some kind. He just didn't understand the nature of it. Before he died, we asked him one question, and one question only. It concerned you, and he was most forthcoming."

A chill spread like cold hands across Wade's back. He jerked on his restraints, to no avail, and decided he might have to try dislocating his arm. "What was the question?"

Cochran stood and checked his watch. "I must be off. The day's only a quarter done. I will, of course, check back in with you later."

"Wait." Wade tried to keep his voice calm, but it was getting difficult. The implications of what Cochran had said about Cartwright nagged at him.

"Yes?" Cochran asked, clearly amused.

"What did Cartwright tell you?"

The old man seemed to consider his answer, then smiled. "Something that proved that the host settings for each subject need tweaking because not every mind is the same, and the ability of a subject to repress memories may be stronger in some than in others."

He nodded his farewell and walked around the table. In frustration, Wade tried to lunge at him, hoping at the very least he might be able to pin the scrawny old man down with his body weight if he timed it just right. But Cochran merely stepped aside and Wade hit the floor, still bound, the dirt floor rough against his skin.

"I'll kill you, you know," he promised. "When this is over—"

"When this is over, Wade, you won't feel the need to harm anyone ever again. And I suspect you'll be referred to as the project's greatest success. They only gave us a month, you know. They gave us August, the hottest month, which suited us just fine. Nothing pushes a man closer to the edge than heat, and entrapment. I think we managed to recreate that scenario quite well, don't you? The pressure, the panic, the cops, the backstabbing friend... "

"The cops...."

"Actors."

"I killed one of them. I saw it."

"You saw a hologram. No cop would be dumb enough to stick his head out knowing you were armed. They would have waited for the SWAT team. You *know* that."

He did, but it hadn't occurred to him at the time. He'd been fighting to survive, to escape. Now it seemed he'd been feeling that way because it was how *they'd* wanted him to feel. They'd played him like a chump from the very beginning, and somehow that, above all else, enraged him. He began to thrash against his restraints, but only succeeded in making the ties slice through the skin on his wrists.

"While you're waiting," Cochran said, and he sounded farther away now, "it might do to ponder something else about this month that's of personal significance to you. I must apologize in advance that we had to condense the experience into what's left of it."

He exited and a moment later, the lights went out. The indigo glow from the television screens was the only illumination in the room.

Behind him, Cochran's voice: "Goodbye, Wade," followed by the sound of a door closing.

He was alone.

* * *

Days seemed to pass him by as he lay on the dirt floor suffocating beneath a sheet of sweat and above a mattress of old dirt. He tried hard not to let Cochran's words drain the fight from him. August was a month that meant nothing. The longer he spent obsessing over it, straining his mind, the less chance he stood of keeping it together long enough to deal with whatever came next, so he banished it from his mind.

Then something on one of the monitors caught his eye. At the same time he was startled by a shriek of static. It quickly abated, fading to a muffled stutter as someone fed audio from the screen he was watching into the basement.

A tall thin man dressed in a dark suit was absently scratching his thigh with the muzzle of a revolver while his other hand turned the hot water faucet in the bathroom sink. The bathroom looked identical to the one in which the phantom child—Eddie—had killed himself, only reversed, like a mirror image. *A simulation*, Wade reminded himself. *That's all it was. Nothing to do with me no matter what that old bastard said. I don't control what other people do with their lives.* Onscreen, the man in the suit leaned over to stare into the sink. The water was exposing something that had been written there, washing away a thin veneer in the basin to reveal a clue, or a message. With great effort, and disregarding the absurd twinge of jealousy that he hadn't thought to do what the man was doing now, Wade tried to straighten his head to make out the words. As it turned out, it wasn't necessary. The man in the bathroom spoke them aloud in a low gravelly voice.

"Revelation."

Beneath the crackle and hiss of the audio, the familiar humming began. To Wade it was like invisible hornets had been released into the room and were coming closer.

The man in the bathroom stopped scratching, set his gun down on the rim of the bath tub, his attention still focused on the sink.

"Repentance."

A noise distracted the man and he turned, made a grab for his revolver, but only succeeded in knocking it into the tub. He cursed loudly as the shower curtain tried to strangle him, and retrieved the weapon. When he straightened, he saw what Wade had already seen. An enormous shadow had darkened the bathroom, cast by someone or something standing on the threshold, just out of frame. Fear contorted the man's face and he jerked out his arm, reflexively and without aiming, pumping one, two, three rounds into the shape before him. The reports were too much for the small speakers to handle. They sounded like a gloved fist thumping a microphone.

Apparently the bullets had no effect. The man screamed and fell back against the sink, cracking his skull against the porcelain rim. He slid to the floor, unconscious.

Allowing Wade to see the final word.

RETRIBUTION

Wade yanked at the restraints so fiercely he felt the flesh bunch up and begin to tear around his wrist bone. He didn't care. He was well able to handle himself, well able to think his way out of damn near any situation, no matter how hopeless it seemed. The pain his efforts incurred was inconsequential in the grander scheme of things. But this situation made him nervous because he wasn't sure what was coming next. The humming was getting louder all the time and the dark was unsettling, obscuring as it would any enemy Cochran might throw at him. Worse, whatever it was would be something from his own head. Something apparently he had forgotten, and what worse monster is there than one with which we are not familiar?

He yanked again and his wrist caught fire. His head swam, lightning bugs sailing through the dark before his eyes. Teeth clenched, he persisted until he felt the zip-tie on one hand slip lower, taking with it a flap of skin. Wade hissed air through his teeth, and looked back at the screens to distract himself from the mounting agony.

The woman with the knife was standing in the living room, watched by a half-dozen indistinct and curiously faceless shapes. They twitched and shook every time she raised the knife and brought it down on her abdomen. At least a half-dozen of them were small, like children, watching impassively, shivering with almost orgasmic glee.

"Fuck," Wade said and redoubled his efforts. Skin tore free, muscles strained, and nerves sang. With a startling burst of pain, his thumb broke with a dull popping sound, but there was no time to consider the injury. Slick with blood and sweat, his hand slipped free of the zip-tie.

"Hallelujah," he said, hoarse from the effort it took not to scream. He took a moment to nail down consciousness as it struggled to leave him, then pulled on the seat of the chair while moving his feet downward. A bit of wriggling and the chair legs were free of the plasticuffs, freeing his own legs in the process. He stood, shakily, his limbs numb, the pain fierce in his right hand. Briefly he inspected it and grimaced. It would need some work, and soon, if he didn't want it to get infected. He had come close to slipping the skin off like a latex glove. The restraint on his left hand proved no easier to remove now that he had all but flayed his right, but eventually he managed to snap the frame of the chair and slide the hand free.

Then he turned to face the screens.

The humming was so loud now it seemed to come from inside him.

Three of the screens had gone dark. Not just blank, they'd been switched off. Wade felt he knew what that meant, and didn't like it much. He felt a modicum of relief that *he* wasn't on one of those screens, waiting to be switched off, then realized he probably was, in some other place, with some other captive watching fearfully on the other side.

Resisting the compulsion to massage the blazing pain from his hand, he used his other hand to search his pockets, his waistband. He was not surprised to find they'd relieved him of his gun, and everything else he'd had on him.

On another of the monitors, a small squat man with a comb over was peering up at the light bulb in one of the upstairs bedrooms while behind him, a black man with half his head missing wriggled like a lizard out from under the sodden mattress.

August, Wade thought as he headed for the door through which Cochran had exited. *The hell happened in August?*

Another screen went blank. Wade could tell only because the blue light from the bank of screens faded a little. It inspired urgency in him. He did not want to be in this musty room when the lights went out.

August...

Despite what Cochran had said, he was sure that particular month held no significance for him. Unwillingly, he ran through a mental list of the people he had encountered and the things he had done over the years. It was difficult, as there had been more than one incident that had occurred during his "gray period", a time in which, like the ill-fated Gail, he had worshipped a chemical god. Of the memories he was able to summon, was not proud, nor could he stand to dwell upon them for long, a development that Cochran might have found of great interest. Wade was not immoral; he did have a conscience. He had just found a way to exist and do what needed to be done without it plaguing him. Regret and remorse were like a pair of mean dogs he kept staked out in his backyard. He knew they were there, but only because he heard them barking, and it was easy enough to drown out the sound.

He found the door. It was made of metal and cold to the touch. There were a number of dents in the surface. Wade scrabbled for a knob and found it, turned, and the door would not open. It hardly budged at all.

"Shit." He hammered on it with his good fist. "Hey!"

To his ears it sounded as if his cry had not gone further than his lips. Meanwhile, the humming seemed to have settled in his ears, those industrious hornets searching for the fastest route to his brain.

His shadow, blurred at the edges, faded as another screen died.

Wade turned. With only a half-dozen screens still on, he would need to find an alternate way out before the room was in total darkness. Quickly, he inspected the ceiling, but saw little, the light blocked by the heavy beams. He recalled how they'd looked in the full light—as if a few tugs would bring them down. It was a risky proposition. If it did come down, he'd be standing right under it and stood a good chance of getting crushed under the weight of its collapse. Another problem was that he was now one-handed and as such doubted he had the strength to cause those rafters much distress.

Sudden frantic motion on one of the screens made him look at them again. Just before it went dark, he thought he saw an obese man try to punch a sobbing woman, until she looked up at him and screamed from the open, fleshless hole of her face.

Wade winced and shook his head, his wounded hand throbbing and dripping blood on the floor. He looked back up at the ceiling. Darker now, the shadows thicker still. *Okay, forget trying to bring it down, he thought.* If it was as fragile as it looked, there was a chance he might be able to use something to knock a hole in it large enough for him to squeeze through. The table would help give him the boost he needed to reach up and pull himself out. Of course, he didn't know where it would lead, but considering his options, it was the better one.

He squinted around the ever-darkening room, eyes scanning the gloom for something, anything he could use, and found only the broken remains of the chair. With difficulty, he braced the broken frame against his chest and kicked out at the legs until they broke away and fell noiselessly to the floor.

Another television went off.

Grabbing one of the chair legs, Wade all but leaped onto the table. It wobbled but held under his feet. He looked up at a dark space between the beams. There was nothing to see there, so he reached up with his unwounded hand and pressed his fingers against the wood. It was soft, spongy and crumbled at his touch. Wade smiled. Perfect. As he'd guessed, it wouldn't take much to punch through, though the space between the beams was going to make it a tight squeeze.

He stepped back, the leg of the chair held like a sword before him, splintered end up, and paused as abruptly, Cochran's words came back to him: *I suggested we build a fully functional neighborhood right in the middle of Harperville's black zone.* Wade frowned, so preoccupied by this newest mystery that he scarcely noticed when another television died. If they had built the neighborhood only recently, why was the basement ceiling decayed, as if it had suffered the weathering of countless generations? The answer, when it presented itself, reduced dramatically the hope that he'd felt at the sight of that crumbling wood.

The ceiling was old and weak because in an otherwise sealed room, it would be the only logical escape route. The decay was deliberate, subtler than a flimsy trapdoor or a neon sign pointing upward, but the nature of it was the same. Like so much of what had occurred since he'd come to Seldom Seen Drive, this move had also been premeditated. Just not by him.

He swore and rammed the chair leg up into the ceiling. It punctured a hole in the wood on the first try. He quickly withdrew the spear and attacked the panel as hard as he could with only his left hand. It was an awkward assault, but the objective was reached. The leg penetrated as if the ceiling were made of bread. With almost manic glee he watched as a hand-sized hole appeared in the wood, lit by the faintest suggestion of daylight.

* * *

The last of the television screens went off and now he was surrounded by darkness that felt dense, heavy, suffocating. The humidity made it seem as if he were in a room with a thousand men, each one struggling to draw air as thick as glue into their lungs. Fresh sweat broke out all over his body. The sound of his blood smacking against the surface of the table was the only sound in the room.

He resumed his assault, jabbing up at the ceiling as if he were Jonah struggling to open a rent in the belly of the whale, every thrust marked by the pained rasp of his breathing.

The air was close, clinging to him.

Wood crumbled. The hole widened.

A television lit up.

Wade did a double take, then glanced over at the screen, guardedly thankful that the cloying dark had been allayed even if only for a moment.

But what he saw on that screen quickly changed his mind.

The picture was grainy black-and-white, the kind of poor quality image generally associated with cheap closed circuit cameras. This one stared unblinkingly down at a wrought iron gate three times as tall as the men waiting in line behind it. A klaxon sounded and the gate swung open, revealing a parade of men in orange jumpsuits, each one with a number printed on the pocket. The majority of the men were black, but here and there a white face was glimpsed, looking distinctly out of place and more than a little scared. Among those faces, Wade recognized a much younger version of his own. He was skinny, his eyes huge dark holes in the round oval of his face. To the adult Wade's older, experienced eyes, he knew the term for a boy who looked like that: "punk" – which meant a prime candidate for rape. The sight of that boy, his face struggling to find a suitably sullen expression to make him appear less vulnerable, sent a wire spinning out from him to his older self, reestablishing a connection Wade had managed to sever in the intervening years.

With the connection, came the memory.

Standing atop the table, Wade exhaled a shuddering breath that took most of his will to fight with it. The arm holding the spear slowly fell to his side, the chair leg clattering off the table. Wade didn't notice. His attention was fixed, not on the video of a younger version of himself entering the maw of hell, but on the time code in the lower left hand corner, which read: 12:15:32 - 8-16-1983.

August 16th, 1983.

Flailing blindly with his one good hand, Wade eased himself down off the table, and moved in an almost dreamlike fashion toward the monitor. Tears filled his eyes as the memories—*cold feet, cold hands, cold walls and warm, heavy bodies, of blood and electric terror, of animal violence, of screaming, of sweat and hate and laughter and loneliness, of hanging bodies, and nakedness, cruel smiles and broken teeth and busted bones, of endless darkness and hot breath in his ear and I'll kill you if you tell*—came to him in a merciless torrent that almost knocked him off his feet.

"Jesus..." he whispered, the humming so loud in his ear now he felt as if something in his brain must surely give. Standing before the screen, trembling, feeling as if everything in him had been scooped out, leaving only a hollow vessel behind, he reached out with his wounded hand and touched bloody fingers to the screen.

The young man tripped over his chains and fell. No one picked him up.

Plenty kicked him while he was down.

The guards did nothing.

A frightened sob burst from the elder Wade's mouth.

And the screen went off.

Darkness crashed back in on him like a wave.

He fell to his knees, mouth agape.

In the dark, someone chuckled.

Cochran's voice came again. Whether or not it was in his head or in the room with him, Wade didn't know, but he could barely make it out over the raging of the hornets.

They only gave us a month, you know...

Wade raised his head. He'd been in prison many times. The longest had been the first time, shortly after his eighteenth birthday. They'd released him from Hell on his twenty-ninth.

Eleven years.

They only gave us a month

And though he remembered every other period of incarceration, he had managed to forget the first, and with good reason.

I must apologize in advance that we had to condense the experience into what's left of it.

Wade stood. He was blind, but as soon as he located the hole in the ceiling he would run to it and get out. He promised himself he would. He was not afraid. No. He could handle himself. He didn't have to run, but enough was enough. Cochran had made his point and he would tell him so and endure the old man's piety for however long it took until this fucking charade was over.

Already he could smell them.

He swallowed, felt his way toward the table.

It was gone.

No. *How?*

Keep it together keep it together keep it together. They're visions, holograms, images. You could walk right through them if you wanted to. They're not real.

Relief then as his hip collided painfully with the table's edge. He had misjudged it in the dark. He almost laughed, but couldn't quite summon the air required. He was drenched in sweat, could hardly breathe. The room had become a sauna, and a foul-smelling one.

In the dark, he heard them pacing.

Wade dropped to his haunches, his hands like antennae, searching the floor for the chair leg. He didn't need a weapon. It would hardly do much good against an immaterial thing, but he wanted it, knew it would make him feel less vulnerable.

They can't hurt you, he reminded himself.

A klaxon sounded in the room, and he cried out in fright.

Gates opening.

No, not gates.

Cell doors.
Keep it together, it's a trick, just a trick, just—
In the dark, someone touched him.

MIDLISTERS

MIDLISTERS

Murder.

It was just a word.

A word I used in my work on an almost daily basis. And if I wasn't actively employing it as a device to dispatch a character, I was thinking about the best way to do it. Envisioning it. Using the people that shuffled around me in Wal-Mart as Crash Test Dummies. Wondering how that old man would fall if a poker came down on his head from behind. Or how that obese lady would shriek if a machete were thrust into her sizable midsection.

The slacker with the sledgehammer.

The clerk with the carving knife.

The bag-boy with the baseball bat.

The look in that infant's eyes as his mother's head plunks into the cart while she keeps pushing for at least a few feet.

And so on and so forth.

Or maybe, in the mood for subtlety, I shied away from the graphic, the grue, the gore, because the scene demanded something quieter. Then again, maybe the story had been quiet (a little...too...quiet...), and graphic was exactly what was needed.

What to do, what to do. Minimalist, or full-on fucking Pollock in his red period? Whichever. It had to be something for the readers to savor and the critics to remember. Something for my fans to disseminate while I sat at inexpensive tables in out-of-the-way bookstores, my cramped hand splayed out, pinning down the book, the cover peeled back to expose the tender flesh beneath where some faceless person I would never meet had tattooed my name. I would try to look interested, try to keep from agonizing over whether or not the greasy-haired kid with the retainer and beads of spittle nestled in the corners of his mouth actually bought my book new or if that leprous bald patch on the cover was the handiwork of the book's original owner, who ripped the price tag off with nary a second thought right before they went and sold it on eBay for a quarter of the original price. But in the end, the scowl always stayed a smile, even if it was more like a wound the doctors couldn't quite figure out to heal; I'd nod in all the right places, endure the kid's animated, probably forced enthusiasm, and scratch my name on the skin of my soul a second time.

The kid would leave happy, maybe tell his buddies he met me and I'm a nice guy, if a little bit on the creepy-looking side. I'd be left with the mystery. His book or not? eBay or ABEbooks. Half-Price Books or the CVS Bargain Bin. Invariably, I'd realize the futility of trying to figure it all out, the folly of caring, and go back to the story in mind.

Back to murder.

As more beaming faces slid into view, and a book, maybe a dozen of them were shoved in front of me, I'd keep that plastic smile going for the benefit of all concerned, while behind my eyes I was a serial killer, sicker of course than I could ever have the capability to be, running down my latest blonde big-breasted victim. Listening to her screams, watching her fall, bearing down on her in all my faux psychotic tiresome misogynistic glory. There might be chainsaws; there'd certainly be blood, and everyone would leave with a grin. And no one ever said my work was without merit. Know why? Because I wasn't Hollywood, and I got a free pass because I wrote literature. I got a free pass because the murder in my books was still just a word.

Make-believe. It meant nothing.

Until it happened for real.

* * *

His name was Kent Gray, and for a long time I hated him. No, I didn't hate him. I fucking loathed the guy. And while, during my occasional visits to his online forum and various other literary message boards I eloquently and reasonably defended my disgust for his work, backing it up with solid examples why everyone else should feel the same way, and being ever-so-careful not to let my hatred of the man himself bleed into my criticism (which given our respective positions on the career ladder would have meant a couple of months of weathering emails loaded with suggestions on how the Kama Sutra, my grandmother and some Astroglide would make for a great evening's entertainment), the truth was I envied him, greatly. And it was not an envy that sprung from something glamorous. He didn't attend premieres of the films they made from his work with the kind of women I would never have draped over his arm. Nothing like that. For starters, despite his success in the literary realm, they never made a movie of his work. They should have. There was no good reason I could see why they didn't (though slow agonizing torture couldn't have pried that opinion out of me on a public forum). But, despite plenty of it being optioned (the announcements of which I had to endure ad infinitum from those troglodytes on his goddamn website message board), nothing ever made it to screen. Kent didn't care, as he so graciously informed his ravening fan base. In fact, according to him, he preferred to have the "integrity" of his work "untainted by Hollywood's convoluted sense of story," whereas I would gladly have donated one of my balls if it meant some fresh-faced cocaine-snuffing fuckwad at Paramount would even glance askew at something with my name on it.

Even the reviews of his books were nothing special. He seldom got raves, but negative reviews were rarer still. There was always something, that great messy unidentifiable something that made everybody like his work on some level, and by default, it endeared them to its creator. And most importantly, in the eyes of those who decide whether or not we'll be paying the gas bill for the next few months, he was a steady seller. His erotic science fiction novels always managed to hold a place, outside the realm of the heavy-hitters like Sting-King and Snora Roberts and Evanobitch, but not far enough down for him to feel my breath on the back of his neck, or to be concerned that anything I threw with my good arm would come anywhere close to grazing him.

He wasn't much of a public figure either, though how much of that was PR, designed to guarantee standing room only whenever he did do a signing, or show up at a benefit for some noble literary function, is anybody's guess. Fact was, you didn't see his handsome smiling mug all over the place, or on billboards flanking highways famous for bad traffic, so chances were you'd have no choice but to sit there sweating and choking on your own cigarette smoke while his fat head beamed down on you with smug approval. He wasn't rich, another misconception he gleefully obliterated.

And for such honesty, he was really the only reliable source. God knows you can't find out these things on the streets, where the general buying public assumes that if there's a book in Barnes & Noble with your name on it, it means you must have the key to the literary equivalent of the executive washroom. They see you and immediately become starry-eyed zombies, their brains assailing them with alert messages that they have found themselves in the company of greatness, which in today's society means someone who has been on TV or the newspapers (celebrity or notoriety doesn't matter—those terms have become interchangeable.) Kent "got by," as did I. We both managed to earn enough to keep ourselves afloat. That, and a basic love for what we did, or a love we used to have for what we did, was one of the only things we had in common. That, and fear, but I'll get to that later.

So, he sold better than I did. His reviews were better. He had a greater readership. More enthusiastic fans. In the weeks before the Aurora Convention where we met for the first and last time, my (worryingly, at times) frequent Google searches on his name turned up at least sixty more pages than mine. His website was more expensive, more accessible, and uncontaminated by pop-up ads. His publisher believed in him, and so gave his books an enthusiastic push. Physically, he was in better shape. He was good-looking, had more hair and better teeth.

Plenty to hate, right? Plenty to invoke ire and envy in equal measures. Hell, maybe you're a writer who lost out on a few awards to the prolific Mr. Gray. If so, envy shouldn't strike you as a radical, unreasonable reaction. I'd hardly be the only guy in that particular self-help group.

But that's not it.

None of those qualities made me hate him with the intensity that kept me awake at nights and left me with the kind of creative impotency that can drive most sane men mad, or to murder, whichever occurs to them first and goes untreated. No, my envy had a simpler, less cosmetic basis: I hated Kent Gray because he was a better writer.

* * *

Gray was, in fact, the kind of writer I had dreamed of being since my early teens when I found myself up to my elbows in Jules Verne, Wells, Hodgson, Lovecraft, Poe, and Blackwood, thick oversized and wordy volumes I had cadged from the library using my mother's card. Up until she died last year, my mother liked to reminisce about how for a long time she thought the skin on my father's face was made from newsprint (Black and White and Read All Over, haw-haw), and mine was a garish palette of ever-changing monstrosities. Such a remark might have had a profoundly adverse effect on my self-confidence, had I not known she was referring to the covers of those Weird Tales magazines I read at every available opportunity, starting at the breakfast table and ending in my bedroom, beneath the covers with a flashlight (clichéd, I know, but no less true). There are huge banks in my memory, saved on my cerebral hard drive and labeled Age: 12-15, in which nothing exists but fond memories of my escape into those dusty tomes and cheap horror comics. You might keep your recollections of your first kiss, your first broken bone, or the first time you jacked off to Linnea Quiqley's naked graveyard dance in *Return of the Living Dead 2* on the top of the stack, but for me, it was all about the words, the stories, and how I would someday use them myself to create the kinds of worlds that offered me an exeunt stage left from the banality of middle-class life. I read on, and I read more, and the passing of time was measured only by the quality of light through the small window in my room. Inevitably, my social skills began to atrophy and in school my grades developed an irresistible attraction to the bottom of the curve. Whenever my mother poked her head in to check that I was studying, she nodded her approval at the sight of the massive science textbook clamped between my grubby hands, little knowing that it was a screen concealing from view the latest *Shadows* anthology.

As my appreciation grew, and the shaky buds of my writing talent began to unfurl, parent-teacher conferences became more frequent.

My mother would sit across the table from my math teacher, arms were folded all over the place like knights reluctant to wield their weapons in the presence of a minor, and I was discussed as if in failing at school, I'd become incorporeal. The only time I got to relax was when my English teacher, a cross-eyed, bushy-haired, but fiercely passionate old guy by the name of Hanson (no relation to the generic pop-culture trio of prepubescent yodelers, thank God), made my mother blush by raving about my potential so enthusiastically, both of us ended up dabbing his spittle from our faces on the way to the car. Hanson called me a "natural-born storyteller with an ear for dialogue" and told her to buy me books instead of clothes or records from now on. It would be, said he, nothing less than an investment in my future. And she did, but the continued erosion of my other grades always countered her pride. As did my father's contention that a life spent living in my own head and making up stories was akin to a life on the breadline. "You want to lie for a living?" he said once. "Become a lawyer. At least you'll get paid for it."

By this time I was fifteen, so while I couldn't yet count telling him where to stick his opinions among my privileges unless I wanted my jaw broken, I was stubborn enough and secure enough in my goals to not let my father's disdain or my mother's uncertainty prevent me from doing what I felt I was born to do. I made friends and lost them when they realized we shared no common interests. While they were chasing ass and alcohol, I was chasing participles and publication, which managed to elude and taunt me, and sour my disposition well into my twenties, by which time I had taken on and left a variety of mind-numbing jobs and temporary girlfriends (though in truth, most of the women in my life left me, and not the other way round, despite my periodic claims to the contrary).

Eventually, six weeks before my twenty-sixth birthday, I came home from my latest stint as a security guard for a briny abandoned warehouse on the docks near my apartment, to find awaiting me a slim white envelope bearing the return address of a magazine I had sent a story to almost a year before.

I didn't even bother opening it.

I got drunk first, then opened the six bills that had been padding the floor beneath that letter. I might have cried a little as I watched my paltry paycheck vanish in a whirlwind of overdue notices. I might even have seen the ghost of my dad—who wasn't dead at the time (that wouldn't happen for another few years), but might as well have been for all I saw of him—sitting in the ratty armchair across from me in my damp anorexic apartment, shaking his head in disappointment.

So I cried, and I beat the living shit out of that chair until I was sure I'd broken a bone in my hand and the chair had coughed up what little guts it'd had when I'd bought it at a yard sale, then I snatched up the letter, tore it open so angrily I ripped the contents in half, and tried to focus on what was undoubtedly the latest in an apparently bottomless well of rejection slips.

I don't know how long I stood there squinting and sniffling at those shreds of paper before it dawned on me that one of them was a check, but when it did, I think I very quietly, very calmly went to the bathroom and threw up a half-bottle of cheap whiskey.

* * *

That check, for the princely sum of $122.07, from the editor of *Eldritch Echoes* (now defunct, but not, I like to think, because they ran my story), saved my life, and certainly my mind. I can look up from this screen right now and it's there, framed on the wall over my desk, slightly yellowed from being in the sun over the years, which gives it a healthier pallor than my own. I should have spent it the very next day. I needed to spend it. After all, that story, written in two days, and edited over one, had earned me roughly half what I was getting for a full week's shift at the warehouse. I should have used it to pay bills, or to celebrate. Instead I taped the check back together, tacked it to the wall (which I wish I hadn't—that tiny hole in the top of the check somehow diminishes the mystique) and sat down with the acceptance letter. It was short, and sweet:

Dear Jason, thank you for...blah, blah, blah...We found your story very...blah, blah, blah...and would like to run it in our October issue. Please find enclosed a check...

No bills were paid; no celebrations ensued. I stayed in, put the check on the wall, and sat down at my piece of crap Olivetti typewriter to write some more. More rejections than acceptances followed over the coming months, but that didn't matter. The first acceptance had proved to me that the voice in my head—the one that coexisted with the muse but was decidedly less supportive, created as it was in some dank laboratory from the limbs of my father's cynicism and the flesh of my own self-doubt and insecurity— hadn't been a crazy one, destined to guide me to failure, poverty, and probably suicide.

I worked, I came home, I wrote. My father's ghost stopped visiting me.

A year and a half after that, on the subway, I first met the woman I would marry.

A month later saw the release of my first novel, *Cutters Inc.* The check for that one isn't on my wall. I saved it for a while, then used it to buy the engagement ring and to finance a down payment on a house. Nothing fancy, or remarkable, just a place that didn't have a bathroom we'd have to share with flatulent neighbors, and where two people could co-exist without killing one another.

For the first time since that childhood time spent lost in the worlds of long-dead writers, I was truly happy.

Then I discovered Kent Gray, and paranoid insecurity, and my life went to pieces all over again.

* * *

My wife was at work when I got the call.

It was winter. We were long enough moved into our house to feel comfortable there, but not long enough to know where everything was, or to be sure the movers hadn't busted and stashed anything. Some of my books and clothes were still in boxes, but there was no hurry. Nobody was going anywhere.

Or so I thought.

Kelly was a schoolteacher at the local elementary. I wasn't quite able to support us both on my income, though sales figures for my third novel, *Black Ribbon 'Round Her Neck*, were good enough that it might be possible soon. Nevertheless, if we'd had to, we could have scraped by, but Kelly didn't work because she had to. She enjoyed the kids, whereas I didn't even enjoy hearing about them. Give me ten minutes in a classroom with a bunch of shrieking hyperactive third graders and I'm liable to rupture something, or someone. But I played the part of the husband well, seemed to have a surprising aptitude for it, as a matter of fact. Plus I loved her, so listening and faking interest while she enthusiastically regaled me with details of her charges' exploits became a necessary ritual, and one I knew was important to her, just as boring her to death with details of my work and the business surrounding it was something I needed her to hear, needed to tell her, even if logic suggested there was no valid reason why she should care about any of it.

Heavy snow made a staticky TV screen of my office window, the white world out there bland enough not to distract me from the task at hand—the seventh chapter of my newest novel *A Time of Good Shear*. The words were coming hard and fast and murder was proving easy when the phone rang. Cursing at the interruption, I forced the end of a sentence that up until the shrill intrusive sound hadn't required conscious thought. I was "in the zone" as those nauseating fitness gurus like to say. With a sigh I pushed myself away from my world, away from the desk and trudged to the phone, which sat like a fat black cat atop the back of the leather couch, waiting for someone to mount it on the wall where it belonged.

I collapsed onto the cushions, and reached behind me to snatch up the receiver, then pinned it between my jaw and shoulder while I reached for the paperback spread-eagled on the floor beside me.

The cover was slick, tasteful. All white, with the silhouette of a naked woman in cobalt blue on the right, a man's sparkling eye superimposed on her back. On the left, a cerulean alien sunrise. Above the artwork, in large blocky raised lettering, was the author's name: KENT GRAY, and beneath, in smaller similar font, the title: CYCLOPEAN HEART.

"Hello?" said a woman's voice into my ear.

"Yeah, sorry. Hi."

"Is this Mr. Tennant?"

"It is."

The book wasn't mine, rather something Kelly had picked up on her last trip to the store. She was an avid reader, thank God, or we'd never have tolerated one another, but her taste in material was pretty awful, to me, anyway. But then, it would have been.

"Sorry to bother you, Mr. Tennant."

"You're not."

"My name is Audrey Vassar. We exchanged some emails recently?"

I looked from the book to the wall and narrowed my eyes. After a moment, it came to me. "Aureoles, right?"

"Aurora," she corrected. "The New England Aurora Convention."

"That's right. I'm sorry."

"I'm calling to ask if you'd be interested in attending this year's convention as a guest of honor?"

I set the paperback down on my chest, and blinked. "Guest of honor?"

"Yes. We've already booked George R.R. Martin, Kent Gray, and a number of other prominent writers in the science fiction field."

I picked up the paperback again, inspected it a little more carefully this time.

"This year," Audrey continued, "in response to some criticism from attendees, we've decided to branch out a little and include some horror writers in our lineup. You know, to see how it goes, with a view to making it a permanent thing."

"Right." Nothing like being made to feel special. Funny thing is though, I did. I'd watched people I considered lesser writers appear at conventions all over the place for so long I was starting to develop a complex, and here at last I was being offered a piece of the pie. Not that it meant a whole lot at the end of the day, and it certainly wasn't going to do my career a lick of good, but what you learn after as many years as I've spent in this business is that the little things count. They count as good things when everything else is deep-fried diarrhea in a basket. Things weren't that bad at the time, weren't bad at all, but my pride and vanity could be pretty high maintenance at times.

It didn't take long for that tiny malformed butterfly of excitement in my stomach to morph into a dollar sign. Not that I was expecting much in the way of compensation. What worried me was our already shaky bank account. Our heels hadn't even cooled in the new house yet, and I wasn't sure I could spring for a trip to Baltimore, so I asked, "And what does this entail exactly, expense-wise?"

"Free room and board for the weekend. Your meals will be covered, and we can offer you $300 toward your flight."

Fuck the flight, I thought immediately. *I'll take the money and drive my ass up there.* And then: *But I bet they offered Martin and Gray a hell of a lot more than that. Maybe even a first-class ride on an air-o-plane built for two.*

"Go on," I urged, and she did.

"We would of course issue free weekend passes to the convention itself for you and a guest, and though we encourage participation in at least one panel, you're certainly not under obligation."

No kidding, I thought. "So when is this?"

"The last weekend of this month."

"This month. That's not much notice." I made it sound as if I was mulling it over, when really I was looking around the room and wondering why the hell I'd agreed to let Kelly paint my office sky blue. Blue. Maybe a cobalt blue woman with a peeper in her back would break the monotony of it. I made a mental note to ask Kent Gray's opinion if I met him at the convention, the name of which I'd forgotten already.

"Mr. Tennant?"

"Yes, sorry, I was just checking my schedule."

"If it doesn't work for you, I'll underst—"

"No, it does," I said, maybe a little too hastily. "And if it turns out I have a conflict, I'll put the other thing off. But for now, yes, pencil me in." Maybe I went a little too far there, but hell, it wasn't like I was accustomed to this sort of thing. At that time, rained-out book-signings at Waldenbooks and apologetic glances from store clerks who mispronounced my name Tenn-*ant* like it was the opening couple of beats of the *Pink Panther* theme song was about all I'd had to deal with.

"Great, I'll put you down, and email you the rest of the information, if that's okay."

"Sure. Thanks."

"Thank you, and I look forward to seeing you there."

She hung up, and so did I, but then immediately dialed my wife's work number to inform her of the news.

The school receptionist answered with her usual fly-in-a-megaphone drone. "Halliwell Elementary School. Linda speak—"

Excitement drove me to interrupt and penetrate the purple-rinse beehive of a haircut my imagination conjured up for "Linda" with my request sooner rather than later, or before her sonorous voice knocked me unconscious. "I need to speak to Kelly Tennant please. It's an emergency."

What I wasn't expecting to hear was: "I'm sorry. Mrs. Tennant isn't here."

"Isn't . . ? Then where is she?"

"At lunch."

I checked my watch. It was lunchtime all right. A half-hour in.

"Do you know where she's having lunch?"

"I'm not allowed to—"

"Sorry, what I meant to say is: Is she having lunch at the school? In the cafeteria, or wherever it is you people eat."

"No, she's not on the premises, but I'm not allowed to say where—"

"This is her husband."

"I understand, sir, but school policy—"

I hung up. Dialed Kelly's cell. I wasn't mad, wasn't frustrated, just impatient to share news few people would or could appreciate. In truth, my wife probably wouldn't either, not like I did. All it would mean to her was that it meant something to me, and that would be enough. It was one of the many reasons I loved her. I felt a rush of excitement at the same time the dial tone ended and her voice, slightly distorted by static, came on the line. "Hey you."

"Hey," I said. "You at lunch?"

"I am. I was just going to call you."

"Good timing. Hey, where are you? Maybe I can get my fat ass down there before you're back in class."

She laughed, my favorite sound in the world. "That would be a little odd, wouldn't it?"

"What do you mean?"

"The kids, sitting around us while we canoodle in the cafeteria. I'd never hear the end of it."

My heart became the school bell, rung a single time, the vibrations traveling through me, as if I'd fallen asleep on a bus with my head against the glass. "You're in the cafeteria?"

"Yeah, why?"

"I just called the school. They said you were out."

Silence for the briefest of moments, but it may as well have been an hour because it shouldn't have been necessary. There was no need for a pause for thought, which I suspected had been just long enough to compose a quick lie. I held the phone away from my ear for a moment, not entirely sure why I was doing it, but it felt like the appropriate action, as if her untruth might deafen me, and looked around the room through eyes that seemed to take a split-second longer than usual sending the images to my brain. All I could think was: *We're married six months. We moved here from nowhere. We're happy.*

She loves me. She's not the type. She wouldn't do this. You're being a moron. But forget ye not that for many years I had dated girls I didn't pay attention to, and treated their duplicity with indifference because I had no emotional investment in them, so I knew it when I saw it, or heard it, or didn't hear it. The difference here was that I did care about Kelly, and didn't like one bit the cold feeling that was worming its way through my guts in the vacuum of her momentary pause.

"I was out," she said. "I just got back."

"From where?"

She scoffed, and the hole she was digging breached the water table. "Marco's. With a few of the teachers."

"Which ones?"

"Why the third degree?"

"Just taking an interest."

She sighed, and it rumbled over the phone. "If you're having a tough day at the keyboard—"

"I'm not. I just called because I had news."

"Yeah? What is it?"

I know it sounds childish, but the taut, defensive tone of her voice in the wake of my inquisition left me unwilling to tell her. My enthusiasm was gone, the butterfly flutter of excitement pounded down into dust. I'm a natural skeptic, a natural cynic (in case that hasn't been made obvious) but I'm also reasonable. I try not to jump to conclusions, and really, in the short space of time I'd been on the phone with my wife, there were any number of them I could have jumped to before the worst one. But I didn't, maybe because everything had been going a little too well and I half-expected something to go wrong.

"Forget it," I told her, sourly. "I'll tell you when you get home."

"Are you all right?"

Peachy. "I'm fine. Talk to you later."

"Okay. Love you."

"Yeah. Me too."

She should have pushed, insisted on hearing the news I'd called to tell her. That she didn't only added to the crawling feeling that something had gone terribly wrong, that our union, which I had been content to let sail along as it was, had, without my realizing it, entered choppy waters.

* * *

Her next mistake was in coming home right on time after school, something she never did. In doing so now, she only proved to me that whatever ordinarily delayed her, it wasn't anything that couldn't wait. Which meant, she stayed late by choice, or for some other reason I wasn't privy to.

She entered the house bundled up in a thick dark brown coat with light brown fur collars and cuffs. The former hue matched her hair, the latter, her skin. I was where I usually am—at my desk, if not writing, then perusing various online message boards, or doing research (all right, I added that last part to make me sound more interesting. I don't do research. If I come upon something I don't know enough about, I make it up).

"Hey," she said, stamping snow from her boots.

"Hey." I didn't look away from the screen. Instead I clicked onto a message board I knew was dark, so I could watch her reflection.

"You eat yet?"

"No."

"Hungry?"

"A little."

"I'll make us something then."

"How was your day?"

"Good. Yours?"

Jesus, we were like office workers with adjoining cubicles instead of husband and wife, exchanging niceties and spinning preamble, all in the hope that this simple perfunctory conversation would delay the inevitable argument.

"It was all right."

I heard the rustle of her hanging up her coat on the stand in the hall, saw in the reflection, her sweater ride up to expose a margin of flesh that despite myself, sent a thrum from my groin up to my sternum. She grew bigger in the screen as she came to stand at the door, arms folded. "Jase?"

"What?" I clicked on a message link, pretended to be interested in what was there to be read.

"Jason."

"What?"

"Look at me."

With a dramatic sigh that made it clear she was asking a lot, I swiveled round in my chair, and folded my arms.

She was smiling slightly, looking absolutely like the beautiful woman I'd met on the subway back in New York, the woman who I'd caught staring at the book in my hands, her head tilted slightly, eyes narrowed as she tried to make out the title. I can't even remember what that book was, and after two seconds of looking at her, I think I might have dropped it. In a bold, uncharacteristic move, I asked her if she wanted to go for a drink. She turned me down. *Quelle surprise*—I'm no Kent Gray—but she did promise to attend the next signing I had in New York. To me, that was as gracious a rejection as I had any right to expect, but a month or so later, at a signing in some crummy side street store in Brooklyn, there she was, with a smile and a copy of *Cutters Inc.* in hand. She later confessed she'd never read anything of mine and harbored a suspicion it wouldn't be to her taste. Coming from anyone else, at any other time, I'd have been disappointed, maybe even a little insulted, but instead her confession encouraged me. After all, if she had no interest in my work, what other reason did she have for being there if not to see me? After the signing we went for dinner, then a drink, then I went back to my ramshackle apartment alone and she returned to the house she shared with her husband. She left him six weeks later, and despite the nagging desire to call her and offer my comforting shoulder and anything else she might need, I held off, exercising previously untapped levels of patience. Three more weeks passed. I buried myself in my work, forcing myself not to think about Kelly, or how much writing time I'd wasted imagining the impossible.

The first weekend of the following month, she called.

Then she came over.

Then we made love for the first time.

Life was good.

"Is that a smile?" she asked, tugging me from thoughts of better times, and I cursed myself for letting it possess me, however briefly.

"Why'd you get so angry today when I asked you where'd you been?"

She shrugged. "I didn't get angry. I just didn't like the sound of the question."

"And how should it have sounded?"

"Like it didn't come from my ex-husband."

I started to say something hurtful in response to that, but trapped it behind my teeth. Instead, I shook my head, and turned back to the screen.

"That didn't come out right," she said, frustrated. "All I meant was that Alex was the suspicious type. I couldn't drive to the grocery store without him asking me who I spoke to, and why I was gone so long."

"And why were you?" I kept my eyes on her reflection, my hand on the mouse, clicking on links that could have been for gopher porn for all I knew.

"Why was I what?"

"Gone so long."

"To be away from him, I guess."

"That why you're doing it now? To be away from me?"

Her reflection suddenly filled the screen. She was right there behind me, her hands on my shoulders. "Can you please look at me when I'm talking to you?"

I did, begrudgingly, turning my chair around to face her. She dropped to her haunches before me, her fingers on my knees.

"Look, you do what you do and you love it," she said. "You can't not do it, and I understand that. You may not believe me, but it's the truth. You also need to have a life outside of it all, though, a life outside of this house."

"Why?"

"To stay sane, I guess. To meet people. To make friends."

"What do I need friends for when I have you? And in case you've forgotten, I spent seven years in an apartment the size of a valise. This house is a serious upgrade in space for me, a goddamn cathedral in comparison, and it's all the room I need. And you are all the company I need."

She stared long and hard at me then, until I had to seriously repress the urge to squirm. Then she shook her head, just slightly.

"Well it's not enough for me."

"What do you mean? You get out plenty."

"Yeah, to work." She rose, walked back to the door, head down as if following her own footprints. Then she turned. "But look what happened today. You called, and I wasn't where I was supposed to be. I stepped out of routine and you went crazy."

Get up, go to her, hold her. Instead I sat and stared. "Crazy? That's a bit harsh, isn't it? And more than a slight exaggeration."

"You know what I mean. It surprised you. And that reaction made me realize where we are. Let's face it, I come home every night and you're still at that bloody computer. You don't have regular work hours. You're always working. I know why you need to be, but I need you too. So if anyone's having an affair," she said, nodding to indicate the computer, "it's you. With that thing."

"When did I say anything about an affair?"

"I'm not an idiot, Jason."

I threw up my hands. "So what do we do about it? You want me to quit?"

"You know I don't. But I also don't want you assuming I'm doing something wrong if I'm not breaking my neck to get home in time when chances are you won't even notice."

I thought about that a moment. She had a point. "Okay."

"And I want to go out more."

"Fine."

"And not always with you."

"With who then?"

"Friends."

"Friends I know?"

"People from work."

"All right."

"Good." She exhaled heavily, ran her fingers through her hair. "It's just that sometimes I need more space than this…cathedral of ours…can offer."

"I understand. Do what you need to."

She studied me carefully, trying to read from my face what she couldn't from my tone. "Are we okay?"

I summoned a smile, the same one I would use in the future for those retainer-wearing slackers at my book-signings. "Yeah, we are."

She returned my smile, closed the distance between us in a few short spaces, then clamped her cold hands to the sides of my face and mashed her lips against mine. I patted her thigh—an awkward paternal gesture—and she straightened.

"I'm starving. Chicken pasta?"

"Sure."

"Great. Won't be long. You can tell me your news over dinner." She disappeared into the kitchen, where I heard pots and pans clattering around, and the swollen pop of a wine bottle being opened.

She sang while she cooked. Happy again, now that our little squabble had been put to bed, and the wrinkles ironed out.

But they hadn't been. Not for me. I loved her and didn't doubt she loved me. I just didn't believe she was telling me the truth. Even after the information she'd volunteered I felt as if there was something she was hiding from me.

Confused, and helpless, I rose and headed for the couch, scooping up *Cyclopean Heart* on the way.

* * *

I got through eighty-seven pages of Gray's novel before Kelly finally hollered at me to wash up for dinner, and I rose in something of a daze, my head filled with images of megalithic spacecraft and pale bookish women in tight latex costumes, and addled by nigh-on impenetrable techno-speak and space-jargon that should have come with a glossary for idiots like me. The story wasn't interesting in the least, but only because it was firmly rooted in a genre I disliked with an intensity that impressed even its bearer. Sex and science fiction might float the boat—or anti-gravity aerocraft—for some, but give me some bare tits, a deformed hillbilly and some power tools and I'm happy. But even though what I'd read of Gray's novel left me with the distinct impression that The Quest to Deflower Abrasively Hyper-Intelligent Pussy on Pluto would have been more apt a title, I was nevertheless alarmed to find myself stricken with a thought usually reserved for the efforts of the masters of my own genre: *Goddamn I wish I'd written that.*

Now, let's be clear about something here: I never have and never will write a space opera, with or without long, rambling but oh-so-poetic descriptions of masturbation in zero gravity or frantic lesbian sex lit by Venusian sunrise. It's not my bag, as they say, so I was far from impressed by Gray's chosen subject matter. Every chapter or so someone lost their clothes and ended up wearing a man or a woman or some alien hybrid with freakishly oversized genitalia instead.

It was ridiculous, and cheap, and he was very, very good at it.

The proof was in my inability to stop reading the damn thing. Even when Kelly hailed me, I speed-read to the end of the chapter I'd been perusing, with an only half-subconscious vow to return to it as soon as I was done with dinner. Had I been tasked with reviewing the book, it might have been one of the most confusing and uneven in recent history. My remarks would be mostly derogatory, with perhaps a quote about how, if my work was often cited as misogynistic, then Kent Gray should long ago have been burned at the stake, which of course would have been a ridiculous and unfair statement, and one I would not have adequate proof to back up should someone contest it. The truth was, despite his stereotypically chiseled male heroes and the apparent reduction of every female character but the elderly (and sometimes even them!) to sex objects, in reality (the fictional reality of Gray's book, that is) the women controlled the worlds and the fate of everyone in them, and though they might gladly throw themselves at the hero's feet, more often than not they were measuring his ankles for shackles, and not the kinky kind.

So guys got to emulate the bronzed ripped hero with the bonus of sex scenes aplenty; the ladies got a well-written love story, with the bonus of sex scenes aplenty, which they would be clever enough to read as manipulation on the part of the female antagonists; and sci-fi geeks got their spaceships, jargon, lusty alien hybrids, and inter-planetary machinations. Plot, myriad subplots, character development, action and romance, all present and accounted for, and all of it detectable in the first eighty-seven pages. All of it written with the same words I used to write my books, only Gray used his as if he'd sat naked on a giant blank canvas for three years, meticulously selecting each and every one until even the most implausible scenes read like poetry. I'd read plenty of books over the years that had left me feeling inadequate, as if the best thing I could do would be to throw my computer out the window and get a job at McDonalds. I'd encountered no shortage of stories, written by folks who'd been active in the field half as long as I'd been, that brought tears to my eyes they were so damn good. So there was no valid reason, at least on the surface of it, why Kent Gray's work should become the sole target of my envy, and Gray himself the focus of my ire. It could have been because his was the work at hand when Kelly "stepped out of routine" and quashed my enthusiasm for what I had been pretending was a less than important deal to me, or maybe it was because what little I had seen of Gray in the cross-genre magazines that were delivered to my door in brown envelopes on a monthly basis, was enough to persuade me he was worth envying, worth hating. Maybe it was nothing more complicated than the presence of his book in my office at the wrong time, left there by a woman I was firmly convinced was cheating on me.

Whatever it was, the seed had been planted.

After a quiet dinner broken only by my announcement of the news, which Kelly greeted with overblown and near-hysterical enthusiasm (no doubt to compensate for crippling it earlier), I took a shower. And later, while Kelly curled up on the couch to watch TV, I sat at the computer and did some research on the man with whom I would most likely be sharing a table at the upcoming convention in Baltimore.

* * *

Ten days later. Audrey Vassar on the line.

"Mr. Tennant, I'm calling to offer my condolences on your loss, and to convey on the behalf of The New England Aurora Convention our sincerest sympathy in this time of—"

"That's very kind of you, Audrey, and I appreciate it, but I'll still be attending."

"Oh. Oh, I didn't..." I could almost hear her quickly changing out of funeral clothes and back into formal. "That really wasn't why I called. We just heard about your father, and wanted to let you know we're here if you need anything."

I couldn't help but grin, and considered asking if she could bring my father back and instill in him the appreciation for me or my career that he'd managed to resist since the very first day I mentioned it. But I'm not that cruel, and though Audrey sounded like a recorded message even when she wasn't trying to offer generic sympathy, I felt no ill will toward her for trying. "Thanks for that. Really. But I'm fine."

"Were you close?"

"Sadly, no."

"That's a shame."

"It is. It is. But what can you do?"

"I suppose that's what it comes down to. I was never very close to my father either."

I cleared my throat—the best way I could think of to indicate to Audrey that although I appreciated her calling, I really didn't have any desire to listen to an account of her own familial dysfunction. Thankfully, she got the hint.

"Anyway, I should let you get back to things. I hope you'll be okay."

"I will, Audrey. Thanks again."

"You have my number."

"I do."

"See you at the convention."

"Count on it."

* * *

My mother came to visit after my father died. Colon cancer had leached the life from him, and though the doctors said he put up a valiant fight, it was my mother's opinion that he'd quit as soon as they wheeled him into the hospital.

"They might as well have given him his last rites right at the door," she told me, with a bitter shake of her head. "Man like Ronald, too good for a hospital, too good for doctors."

"And everyone else," I said, surprised at my own bitterness, which drew my mother's watery gaze up from the floor as if I'd cast a lure into the briny deep and snagged a pair of cold stones. But then she nodded, faintly, and looked at my computer screen, maybe at her own reflection in the glass, or the ghost of all those words I'd hacked out on it, which I suspect she believed contributed to my father's lack of a struggle at the end. *Mrs. Tennant, I'm afraid your husband's gone. Terminal disappointment, it was. Hell of a thing.* Kelly hovered in the background like a beautiful ghost, feeding and entertaining the intermittent visitors, most of whom were from her school and not anyone I knew, there to offer support despite not being fully sure who'd died. More than once I caught myself studying the small crowd, hoping to find among them a viable candidate for my wife's adulterous affection. But there were no lingering glances or intimate touches, no sidelong glances or dry mouths, no hastily severed conversations when I entered the room, no extended periods of absence for Kelly or anyone else. Nothing.

But my attentiveness did not go unnoticed.

"Are you worried?"

I glanced from the crowd to my mother's taut, terribly aged face, then down into my drink. "A little."

"Are things not going well?"

I shrugged, raised my head at the sound of Kelly's muffled laughter. A tall, patrician looking old man with a hawk-like nose and a slicked back skullcap of silver hair was stooped forward, whispering into her ear. And my wife, a hand over her mouth, eyes wide, was listening in shameful fascination to whatever he was saying. Another elderly man flanked her, this one with a shock of white hair rising from a liver-spotted dome of a skull, and a maroon handkerchief poking like a leering tongue from the pocket of his pinstriped suit. He watched his colleague knowingly, anticipating the punch line.

"They're going," I replied, and took a sip from my drink. "I'm just not sure where."

A pained look crossed my mother's face. "She loves you, you know."

"Yeah. I do."

"Then why worry?"

"Because..." I looked back down into my glass, at my eye trapped in amber. The great irony of my being a writer is that outside of the page, I'm not the greatest communicator. Oh I can talk until the cows come home, but very rarely is it anything personal, anything I really need to talk about. Listen to me being interviewed on the radio, or read one in a magazine and you'll see what I mean. All the long answers are about writing. "Because I don't understand why."

And that was the truth of it, even as I watched my mother smile and relax her shoulders in what I assumed was preparation for the great "Is That All It Is? Pshaw, You Silly Goose!" speech.

But instead, "We all question what our partners see in us now and again," she said, clasping her hands together, and checking to ensure Kelly wasn't within earshot. "You know how difficult your father was to live with. You don't know how many times I asked myself why he bothered to marry someone he barely seemed to tolerate at the best of times."

"I can imagine."

"No," she said, her smile turned down at the corners. "No you can't. Not after a few months of marriage, you can't. Give it twenty-five years of doubt and see what it does to you. But this," she said, casting another quick glance at Kelly, "is a good thing, a new thing. You need to give it time, and stop looking for the cracks, because if you look hard enough, you will find them, and you'll pry them wider without even knowing you're doing it. Kelly's a good woman, but you'll only get out of this bond what you're willing to put in." She nodded for punctuation, and sat back.

I did the same, appraising her as I let out a breath that seemed to take half my weight with it. "That's pretty profound, Mom."

"Eh," she said, waggling a hand in the air before her. "Years of daytime TV have to be good for something." She chuckled then, but it was an automatic addendum to her words, tacked on and utterly devoid of sincerity.

How could there have been any genuine mirth to it? My father—long-regarded as an ogre by a punk kid who, when not railing against anything that interfered with his goal of being the next Stephen King, was distributing handwritten, stapled-together manuscripts loaded with decapitations and mutilations to the relatives at Christmas—had been the love of my mother's life. The man I'd feared every time he came home from the steel mill pissed off, a six-pack of Old Milwaukee tucked beneath his arm, wearing a scowl so deep it made tar pits of his eyes, was still the man who had romanced her, taken her dancing, had driven her to Niagara Falls one summer's night to get down on bended knee and ask her to ride shotgun with him to the end of the road.

All my life she'd been a not entirely trustworthy interpreter, turning my father's grunts, sharp gestures, and muttered responses to me into terms of endearment, or encouragement. Even as a child I didn't buy it, but though I appreciated her efforts I'd never understood, and still couldn't, why he'd never cared for me. I'm sure—unless I've repressed the memories—that I never gave him a specific reason to dislike me, to treat me with less respect than he'd offer someone who took his seat on the bus. Unless that was it? Maybe when I'd come along, I'd annexed my mother's affection, inadvertently shutting him out, leaving him to fend for himself and play father to a child he resented.

An alarming thought, and one I quickly stowed. Besides, while children are intuitive, and damn near precognitive creatures—blessed, and often cursed, with the ability to read adults—they can't determine what isn't shown in the eyes, can't follow the trail if they can't see where it begins. My father was a locked door, always. The room beyond a mystery, so anything I might surmise now was little more than speculation, gleaned from dusty recollections and tainted by hurt.

"What are you going to do now?" I asked her, to sever the thread of my own thoughts and divert her attention from my situation.

She gave a long lingering sigh. "Move on," she told me. "What else is there to do?"

"You're welcome to stay here for a while."

"That's good of you, Jason, but you have enough problems without me getting in the way."

"You wouldn't be in the way."

She raised an eyebrow. "Honey, when it comes to situations like yours, parents are always in the way."

"I could come stay with you, you know, for a few days."

She leaned forward, and put a wrinkled hand on my knee. "You're needed here."

Jesus, I thought, *when did she get so old?* I'd made a point of visiting her at least three times a year, outside of holidays which we alternated with Kelly's parents, and had never noticed before how much she'd changed from the picture of her I always saw when she was in my thoughts. I was afraid that one of these days only her voice would be recognizable, everything else loosened around her thin frame like an ill-fitting glove, as if God's Laundromat had returned to her the wrong costume. I was more than afraid; I was terrified and saddened. She had always been a face in the audience, bearing witness to my spotlighted theatrics when the houselights had gone down. Invisible, but there.

I reached out and took her hand. "Thank you," I said, in a low voice.

She looked genuinely surprised. "For what?"

"You know what."

"Well then, you're welcome, for whatever it is."

"And I'm sorry about Dad." I made a point of not specifying just which part I was sorry for—his death, or my relationship with him in life, and she didn't ask me to. We just sat there, exchanging sad smiles, reminiscing a little, and generally catching up. I vowed to call her more, and visit whenever I could. She gave me a look that suggested it was nice of me to say, but we both knew it would last only until I was sure she wasn't going to wither away now that the sunlight my father had represented in her life had been snuffed out.

"I want you to do me a favor," she asked me the night she left. "It's not an easy one."

She had been about to leave, standing on the threshold of the icy dark, her car waiting like a giant frozen cockroach by the curb. I urged her back inside, shut the door on the cold, and waited for her to continue. Kelly had been standing in the kitchen doorway, after dispensing the requisite sympathy and offers of assistance, one last time. Now she silently pushed away from the jamb and disappeared into the other rooms, leaving us alone.

"I want you to remember him as a good person," my mother said, her liquid blue eyes searching mine, conveying the plea. "Because he was. He just didn't know how to be a father. It wasn't in him. Doesn't mean he didn't love you."

Had she said this in my father's company, he'd have scoffed and left the room, and I'd have muttered something insulting. Two guys cursing a stubborn tree stump, but making no attempt to move it. But he wasn't here. We'd buried him, and if this was what my mother needed to be happy for however many years she could manage without him, I would give it to her. So though I had trouble with the idea, and suspected it wouldn't take even if I gave it the 'ol college try, I nodded, gave her a hug that only brought home to me just how truly frail her body had become—it was like embracing a stack of kindling wrapped in burlap—and saw her to the car.

* * *

That night I couldn't sleep, and when I went downstairs to get a drink of water, maybe check my email, I found my dead father sitting in my office, in that busted up old chair from my apartment—a chair I'd left there when I'd moved. He was by the window, lit by slats of light from the streetlamps through the blinds, what little hair he'd had in those last few years of his life tousled as if he'd just woken.

I froze in the doorway, waiting to wake up, waiting to scream, waiting for him to speak.

But he didn't. He just sat there like some cruel mortician's idea of a joke, waxen-faced, and glassy-eyed.

Shaking his head.

It was the whiskey, of course, and whatever residual grief I'd tried to repress, but regardless, I snuggled up tight with Kelly when I went back to bed, so tight in fact that she had to pry herself free of me at one point, and turn around so that she could hold me and still manage to breathe.

In the morning we made love, just to reassure ourselves that the passing of my father hadn't broken the gears of the universe, that though the light might look less bright and the angles a little sharper, he had left the world more or less as he'd found it for those who'd survived him.

* * *

I drove to Baltimore alone. It was my choice. And though Kelly had been surprised when I announced my intentions, I could sense her relief, and for that I couldn't blame her. I wasn't much looking forward to it. The excitement I'd felt at having been asked had long ago evaporated. Not solely because of the other circumstances that made that day one to remember, or my father's death shortly thereafter, but because since then I'd had nothing but time to realize the bother and hassle these conventions generally represented. It was an arduous trip too, through slushy roads and barren monochrome landscapes that, if they hadn't already been mirroring my emotional state, would have depressed the hell out of me. More than once I considered swinging the car around and going home, but was kept moving forward by the awareness that there was little back there to look forward to but my own self-pity, and that guy was already taking up too much room in *chez* Tennant. So I drove on, distracted every now and then by the chirp of my wife's cell phone, which she'd given me so I wouldn't have to fight my way through crowds at the convention to let her know I was okay.

"You're not too far to think about coming back to get me, you know," she said, her voice mangled by hiccups of static.

"I know, but even if you sit around the house just staring at the wall, it'll still be more interesting than this is going to be."

"Don't say that. Try to think positive. You might have fun."

"Yeah."

"Oh, and I've a bone to pick with you."

"Uh oh."

"Yeah. You were reading my book, right? The Kent Gray one?"

"I was. It was trashy."

"Maybe so, but since when do you draw all over books? I thought that was a big no-no for writers. Makes 'em all crinkly."

"The books or the writers?"

"Haw-haw. You know what I mean."

I turned on the windshield wipers to liberate the glass from a patch of icy snow. "I was marking the passages I liked. The ones I wish I'd written."

"You're kidding." A staccato hiss followed her words as the connection wavered.

"No."

"You found something to like in that book?"

"Didn't you? You bought the thing."

"The only thing worth looking at was the author photo."

Something in me tightened at that, but I let it go. As I've mentioned, and as you probably know, Kent Gray was a handsome chap. I'm sure most women got a little damp over his photo, so why should my wife be any different?

"I'll be sure to tell him you said that."

"Please do," she replied. "And while you're at it, tell him his sex scenes suck."

I laughed out loud at that, and felt instantly better.

"I much prefer yours," she continued. "But then, I might be biased, since I get to help you research them."

I squinted as a car passed me and kicked up snow. "Thanks babe. Listen, I gotta go. Weather's getting nasty."

"Okay. Well...I hope you sell a ton of books."

At that, I looked in my rearview at the three cardboard boxes loaded with paperbacks on the back seat. It still felt weird schlepping them to a convention, and I could only imagine how ridiculous I was going to look if I had to leave with them still full. How many of the other guests would have their cars stuffed full of books, hoping to make a quick buck? I had to try real hard not to think about it.

"So do I," I told Kelly. "I'll call you when I reach the hotel."

"Drive safe."

I snapped the cell phone closed and tossed it on the passenger seat, then concentrated on the road, which had rapidly become a slippery white ribbon bordered by spindly-limbed trees that seemed determined to grab the car, their ragged fingers scratching at the roof. Occupying my mind with trying to keep the car from sliding into oncoming traffic as vehicles exploded from sizzling sheets of nothingness like wolves from the fog allowed me some respite from the dark shapes lingering on the threshold of consciousness, awaiting consideration. Even when the road widened, and the car finally sprang free of the womb of snow, I turned on the radio to keep my focus on the road and what lay at the end of it. I did not want to think about Kelly alone—or worse, not alone—back at home. I did not want to think about how inadequate and out of place I felt puttering to a convention where the chances were the attendees would be ninety-percent science fiction fans, ten-percent horror, with that ten-percent unaware that anyone but King, Straub, Barker and Anne Rice were writing horror these days

"Knock it off," I chided. I'd be fine, and I reminded myself that if things went sour for me, there was always the option of leaving early. I wouldn't be out a dime and could be home in a few hours. And hey, Kelly was right, maybe pigs would sprout little porcine wings and I might actually enjoy myself, maybe empty a box or two of books while chatting with some enthusiastic readers. Could happen. I dragged a smile from the well of doubt, and held it as I edged ever closer to my destination.

* * *

Fifty miles from the Marriott Hotel, I passed a hitchhiker who'd been holding up a sign with AURORA CONVENTION scrawled on it in thick black letters. The guy had looked young, and cold as hell, but the pang of guilt I felt at spraying him with slushy water was alleviated by the memory of a scene I had written in which a salesman foolish enough to pick up a beautiful hitchhiker had been castrated by her with a straight razor.

I pressed my foot a little harder on the gas, warmed by the heat inside the car and the knowledge that I was on the home stretch. I wasn't concerned about the hitcher recognizing me if he passed me in the packed halls at the convention. I'd been going plenty fast.

Then my tire exploded.

I was coasting along, tapping my foot to a Paul Simon number I didn't even know, but remembered my mother liking once upon a time, when there was a brief, agonized screech, and the car bucked like a startled horse. Snowy gravel machine-gunned the side of the car and the wheel spun abruptly to the right, hell-bent on sending me into a railing at seventy miles an hour. I cursed as I wrestled it into submission, allowing it to stay its course toward oblivion, but jamming on the brakes well before its rendezvous with the railing.

The car squeaked noisily and shuddered to a messy stop, the rear end slipping off the road, so the nose of my Pontiac was aimed at passing traffic, and slightly skyward.

"Fuck." I thumped a fist on the steering wheel, then sat back and closed my eyes. Blindly, I fumbled for the cell phone, and wondered who to call. Were we members of Triple A? Was Triple A even in business anymore? This was the kind of crap Kelly knew, not me; this, and to whom we owed money, when and where the checks were sent, how to cook food without burning it, how and when the taxes were done etc., etc. I figured the best idea was to call her.

She wasn't there.

I stared at the phone, checked the signal, which of course was fine, then hung up and tried again. It rang out, then my own solemn voice advised me to leave a message.

I flung the phone over my shoulder where it smacked against one of the boxes and hit the floor. And scarcely taking the time to check that an eighteen-wheeler wasn't bearing down on me, I stepped out into the road. Fortunately, there were no cars at all, nothing but the nut-preserving chill that made my teeth irresistible to each other and induced rigor mortis in every hair on my body.

"Chriiiist," I moaned as I hugged myself, and in the kind of half crouch reserved for the old, the cold, or the constipated, made my way around the car to inspect the damage. It took only a moment to locate the offending tire, or rather, the wheel, because the tire itself had said its goodbyes and blown the pop stand without so much as a note. I imagined it was back there, lying in the middle of the road like rubbery roadkill, still managing even in death to inconvenience others.

Pissed off, though not in the least bit surprised (for this was just another of those things which occur with semi-regularity and can be blamed firmly on whatever deity has been squatting over me, pants bunched around His ankles, all my life). To think about Kelly at that moment, and where she might be, who she might be with, and what they might be doing would have meant the utter annihilation of my car. I'd have torn it asunder with my chattering teeth, then torched the remains. So I let the anger keep my thoughts on stir-fry as I wrenched open the car door, tugged the keys free of the ignition, stalked around to the back of the crippled vehicle, and yanked open the trunk.

Against all my expectations, and therefore confusing me a little, there was a spare in the trunk, in relatively good shape too, nestled next to the tools required for the job. I stared at them through the clouds of my breath for some indeterminate amount of time before a voice made me jump so violently, I almost lost my footing.

"Jesus Christ." Whirling to face the speaker, I realized he would never know just how lucky he was that I hadn't already plucked the tire iron out of the trunk.

"Hey sorry, man, sorry," the guy said, hands raised to ward off the blow I was imagining for him. I put a hand to my chest, though there was nothing wrong with my heart. My lungs maybe, but not the ticker, which wasn't where it should be anyway but in my throat, busy blocking off the air I needed to suck in to tell this guy what I thought of him. When at last I felt the panic and anger ebb, I realized I was looking at the hitchhiker I'd sloshed by earlier, nothing but red cheeks and watery eyes visible over the thick black woolen scarf he'd wrapped around his lower face. A stocking cap was pulled down over his ears, but despite the padded jacket he wore, he looked half a hopscotch step from hypothermia. The sign I'd seen him holding aloft lay forgotten and fringed with snow at his feet.

"Didn't mean to freak you out, man," he said, waggling his hands in some lazy estimation of my panic. "Just wanted to know if you needed help."

With my breathing regulated just enough to allow me to form complete sentences without keeling over, I nodded pointedly at the spare. "Tire blew out."

"Yeah, I saw it back there. You were lucky."

"You know anything about changing one?"

"Only that it's what needs to happen after one of them explodes."

I closed my eyes. "But not how to facilitate its replacement, right?"

He shrugged. "I could help you push it."

I gave him a withering look. "Where?"

Another shrug, and now I began to seriously consider getting the tire iron out anyway. "You headed to the convention?"

"I was, yeah."

He nodded his approval. "Me too. Came all the way from Ontario."

I straightened, appraised him as I would a dog that had just spoken fluent Italian. "Ontario?"

"Yep."

"You hitched all the way here?"

Though I couldn't see his mouth, I could sense his smile as he produced a gloved thumb and stuck it out. "Sure did."

"Why?"

"Haven't got any money, man."

"No, I mean, why come all this way just for a convention?"

I knew what he was going to say a moment before he said it, and wished I hadn't asked.

"Shit, man. It's not every day you get to see Kent Gray in person."

* * *

"Name's Walt, by the way," the hitcher said, removing the glove from his right hand and offering it in my direction.

We were back in my car and moving, after almost two hours spent making runway-cleared-for-landing-type signals at uncaring drivers. Finally one stopped, and a burly guy who I made a note to use in my next inbred-cannibal-psycho story replaced the tire, all the while casting glances at me that I chose to interpret as disappointment in his fellow man.

I shook Walt's hand. "Jason."

"Cool." He rubbed his palms together, then held them up in front of the heater vents. "Hey, thanks for the ride. Who are you going to see?"

"Not sure. I'm a guest. Chances are I'll see everyone."

"A guest? No kidding." He turned sideways in his seat to reevaluate me. Without the scarf, I could see he was older than I'd assumed when I'd whizzed by him, but not much. The lingering traces of acne and the mismatched tufts of blonde beard on the point of his narrow chin told me he had not yet fumbled into his second decade. "So, like, who are you?" He glanced into the back seat. "A writer?"

"Yeah."

"That's cool. What kind of stuff do you write?"

"Horror."

"Cool," he said again, but with decidedly less enthusiasm.

"Have I read anything you wrote?"

I resisted the urge to smack him. "How would I know? I just met you."

He laughed. "Yeah, sorry. I should have said: What are some of your books?"

That was only a slightly less annoying way of putting it, but I told him to reach into one of the boxes and grab the first one that came to hand. Grinning widely, he unsnapped his seatbelt and jostled his lean torso against my elbow, then drew back, a pristine copy of *Cutters Inc.* in hand.

"Seatbelt," I said, and he looked at me oddly for a moment, until I urged his gaze downward.

"Oh right, sorry." He buckled himself back in, then studied the book. I couldn't resist trying to read the expressions that passed over his face, but quickly looked away when he turned to me again.

"Man, this is no good."

I felt like a kid had punched me in the stomach, the kind of punch that doesn't hurt exactly, but definitely registers. "Excuse me?"

He looked at me, and the faux pas dawned on him. Wide-eyed, the book resting on his lap, he raised his hands again and grinned at me from the space between them. "Oh shit, no. Aw, no, man...I didn't mean it like that. What I meant is, this book—" He picked it up again to check the title. "—*Cutters Inc.* What I meant was, it's no good that I picked this one, because I've already read it."

"Yeah?" Some of the ice melted from my lungs.

"Yeah." He shook his head, then went back to looking out the window. I stared at the side of his face until throttling him suggested itself as a good way to get his attention. I know how un-cool it is to ask someone's opinion of your work, particularly when it's supposed to be flattery enough to be told they've read it, and especially if the guy who says he's read it has traveled a million miles to meet his hero, who is not a horror writer, but I couldn't help myself. By saying nothing, he was, whether he knew it or not, implying that he hadn't liked it, that silence was preferable to admitting he thought it stunk. And it would be a shame for the poor guy to unwittingly give me the wrong impression. Unless of course he was lying to be polite and had never read the book, in which case I decided I'd have to quiz him on its contents, just to see him squirm.

"I can't believe I didn't recognize you, man," he said then.

"What?"

He beamed as he hefted the book, displaying the picture on the back cover of a younger, happier-looking me. "Shit, I read this in high school man, and the other one…the one about the serial killer and the hookers…*Red*-something, wasn't it?"

"Yeah." I found myself sharing his smile. "Yeah, it was. *Raw Red Smile*."

"That's the one!" He nodded his satisfaction. "I dug this shit back in college, man."

"Big jump from me to Kent Gray."

"Yeah. Yeah it is. Blame rehab."

"How's that?"

"Only book I could find in there that wasn't a romance, or self-help, or some other crock of shit."

I made a note to periodically distribute copies of my books to rehab centers throughout New York. If my agent caught wind of it, he'd probably tell me I was wasting my time, but I now had it on good authority that it was an effective means of promotion. I even envisioned a poster of me looking all washed out, dark circles beneath my eyes, lips cracked and pale, my hair and clothes in shambles, holding a copy of my book over a caption that read: JASON TENN-*ANT*. THE CRACKHEAD'S CHOICE!

I chuckled at that, then caught myself and glanced at my passenger.

"Well, I'm glad you enjoyed my work."

"Oh yeah. It was good stuff, man. You done more since the *Raw Red* one?"

"One since then. It's in the box. Help yourself."

"For real?"

"Sure."

"That's awesome, man." He slapped his knee as if I'd just cracked a joke. Maybe it was because he had just bought my ego a round, or because we were almost at the hotel, despite the setbacks along the way, but my attitude toward him had thawed considerably.

"Can I get you to sign them for me?"

I mulled this over, until I knew he was starting to worry that he'd offended me by adding a request to a free ride and free books.

He hadn't. I was plotting. "Sure," I said, finally. "But do me a favor?"

"Yeah, no problem."

"Ask me again when we're at Kent Gray's table."

* * *

I guided the Pontiac into the only space not taken, pleased to see that someone had placed miniature cones around it, and hung a small laminated sign on a chain that read: RESERVED FOR J. TENNANT. Still buoyed a little by Walt the Ex-Druggie's flattery, the parking reservation made me happier than it might otherwise have, and I sat for a moment with the engine off, flirting with childish glee until Walt cleared his throat.

"Well man, I appreciate the ride, and the books and everything."

"No sweat."

"I'm going to take off."

"Sure. Don't forget you need those books signed."

Frowning, as if he still couldn't fathom why I had specified the exact location for this to take place, he nodded and scooped up the books—a copy of *Black Ribbon 'Round Her Neck* and *Raw Red Smile*, which he'd requested despite his claim that he'd already read it. "I'll see you later, man. Thanks again."

"Anytime, Walt."

I watched him hurry through the biting cold to the main entrance of the hotel, where a lanky bespectacled guy in heavy clothing stopped to check his ticket, which Walt produced with a flourish. Satisfied, the ticket master stepped aside and went back to looking officious on probably the only day of the year he was allowed to, a feat made easier by the temperature. His demeanor changed considerably however when flashed the guest ID badge Audrey Vassar had mailed me. His red cheeks almost creaked as they rose to accommodate a yellow-toothed smile, and he shook my hand with a vigor that made my fillings rattle before clipping my ID to a festive-looking chain and looping it around my neck.

I entered the warmth of the hotel feeling a thousand leagues more confident than I had leaving the house only six hours earlier, until I remembered I'd left the cell phone in the car. And that got me thinking about Kelly again, and whether or not there was any point in calling her. I decided to preserve my burgeoning contentment, at least for a little while, and try again later.

The lobby of the hotel, not plush and certainly homely, had to be judged by the quality of light, the size of the room, and the ill-glimpsed swatches of pale yellow flocked wallpaper, as the crowd obscured anything that might have impressed. Still standing just inside the door, but off to the side so I could observe without being overtly noticeable, and nestled in a twilight of artificial amber light and winter shadow, I studied the throng of bodies. Despite their number, only a low, almost reverent hum of conversation emanated from the nucleus of costumed folk, who seemed possessed of an animation and purposefulness usually expected of auctioneers at Sotheby's. This energy only served to make the lack of obnoxious chatter all the more incongruous, as if they were waiting for something.

Dispelling all self-deceptive illusions that I might be a contender for their anticipation, I circumvented the crowd and headed for what I quickly deduced was the great haven of all lost men who have woken up to find themselves among aliens and androids in The Androgynous Zone—the bar.

"Jason?"

I had scarcely stepped foot inside, the door still groaning shut behind me, when I found myself being approached with some urgency by an attractive older woman clutching a clipboard. She had pushed away from her place at the long low mahogany bar like a swimmer from a pier, her outstretched hand slicing through the waves of cigarette smoke as she closed the distance between us.

"Jason Tennant?"

I nodded somewhat dumbly, and shook her hand. "Yes."

Her grin widened, now bereft of the slight uncertainty that had been censoring the corners. "Audrey Vassar."

"Ah, Audrey. Hi," I said, allowing myself to relax. "Good to see you."

"Good to see you too." She gave me a charming smile and did a quick hair flip I might have taken as flirtation ten years ago when I had more hair and better teeth, but presumed was slight nervousness now.

For some reason her voice on the phone, which in truth still sounded prerecorded in person, had given me the impression she was in her fifties, overweight, and not particularly attractive, but I was wrong on all counts. She couldn't have been more than forty, and if she was she hid it well. Her light brown suit and cream-colored blouse complemented her hair, which was a lustrous, wavy blonde that fell to her shoulders, where it curled inward in a style that suited her heart-shaped face. She was lightly tanned, and hazel-eyed, with a small mole like a period above her right eyebrow. I couldn't help but wonder if the location of that mole, above rather than below her long thin nose, had kept her from being a model, where it seemed careers were decided based on the position of such things, for she certainly seemed to fit the bill in all other respects.

If she noticed my longer-than-appropriate appraisal, it didn't show on her face, but I checked myself and scratched my jaw.

"Sorry I'm late. Car trouble."

"No problem at all. Would you like a drink?"

"I'd love one."

She led the way to the bar, which I saw was occupied by a peculiar mixture of harried looking men and women—regular guests of the hotel (who looked sorry they'd chosen this weekend to check in): the occasional bouncer brooding over a presumably non-alcoholic beverage while practicing the mean look that guaranteed his paycheck, a couple of teenagers made up to look like sexless creatures from some science fiction show of which I was blissfully unaware, a guy or a girl in a remarkably convincing Chewbacca suit, a pair of youths in black pants and T-shirts, who looked like they'd just finished their shift behind the bar, and a duo of middle-aged men in suits conferring over a stack of papers. There were people in the booths lining the walls around us too, but the haze of smoke and poor lighting in the bar reduced the occupants to muttered voices, coughs, and the occasional clink of a glass.

Audrey leaned over the bar and raised a hand until a morose looking youth with gel-set black hair and an eyebrow pierced with what appeared to be a railway spike from a model train set sighed his way down to us.

"Vodka tonic," she said in that flat no-nonsense voice, and I added "Beer," when prompted. Then, as the maudlin barman tugged his languid gaze from Audrey's ID badge to mine, and set about the apparently strenuous task of fulfilling our order, I waited for Audrey to sit, then joined her.

"I expected to see you lugging a box of your books around," she remarked. "Or have you already deposited them in your room?"

"Nah," I said. "I didn't bring any. Figured anyone who'd be interested would already have them."

She nodded her understanding, then unclamped a sheet of yellow paper from her clipboard and set it before me. "The weekend schedule," she said. "As I think I mentioned before, you don't have to attend anything. It's all optional, though naturally your fans will expect to see you at some stage."

"Let's hope they're all drinkers then," I said, and chuckled. She laughed along a moment later, but there was concern on her face, which I quickly alleviated by telling her I was joking. Even though I wasn't yet sure that was the case.

"We have a panel specifically for horror writers too," she went on, drawing one polished fingernail down the page to Saturday's event schedule. I leaned in close enough to smell her perfume, and saw what she was indicating. HORROR IN LITERATURE: VIOLENCE AS AN ARTFORM. I tried to restrain a wince. "Given the style of your work," Audrey said, "you'd be perfect for this." She raised her hands. "No pressure, of course, but it is within your field of expertise."

Coercion through flattery.

"You've read my books then?"

"Oh no," she said, with a grimace. "I haven't the stomach for that stuff. My husband does though. He's got all of your titles." She reached into the breast pocket of her jacket and produced a pack of Marlboros, one of which I planned to cadge from her until I realized they were menthols. "Interesting covers though," she finished, with a wink. Oddly enough, the impulse to be offended at her obvious repugnance for my work didn't rise as expected. Maybe it was because she'd qualified it by saying her old man enjoyed it, or because she was distractingly pretty. Then again, whenever people tell me they don't like my books and in the same sentence tell me they've never read them, I find solace in the fact that they're repelled by the preconceived idea of what awaits them. That they're probably right doesn't factor into it. At the end of the day, they're really only criticizing the subgenre, and my lurid covers, not the words within. *I don't like your writing* stings a lot more.

"Well, tell your husband he has impeccable taste in literature."

Cigarette lit and already trailing mint-scented smoke from her mouth, she nodded.

The barman arrived and deposited our drinks with an expression on his face like he'd just delivered to us his own organs, and Audrey raised her glass in a silent toast.

"How do you operate a convention while soused?"

She gasped. "I'm not soused!"

"I wasn't saying you were, but it's a bit early for vodka, isn't it?"

"Listen buster," she said, narrowing her eyes, the fake threat offset by her smile. "I'm the only one around here who'll be able to tell when I'm crocked, and for your information, it actually helps to be somewhat out of it at these things."

"Really?"

She took a hearty swig from her glass, then cocked her head at the people around us. "Hell, everybody else is."

Endlessly amused, and more than pleasantly surprised at Audrey's affability, I laughed and took a sip of my beer, my life at home rapidly fading in my mind to a postcard I could set aside to review later, when the company was not so interesting and my head was fogged with alcohol. Let's be clear though, Audrey was certainly attractive, as I have more than made clear, but I had no designs on her, and wouldn't have had even if she'd been single, and interested. In another life, maybe. All right, definitely. But in this one, I was merely enjoying her company, which, considering I'd envisioned a weekend spent floating from room to room enduring the disappointment of fans whose enthusiasm and drunkenness had led them to mistake me for someone else, was certainly a welcome development.

I watched her blow smoke out one side of her mouth, then abruptly her face fell as she caught sight of something over my shoulder. "Shit." I started to turn, but her hand fell on my knee, sending a jolt of not entirely unpleasant electricity up my inner thigh. (Yeah, I know what I just said about interest, but I'm also a guy, all right?) "Don't look," she murmured, and did her hair flip thing again as her smile returned and she beckoned for me to move closer, ostensibly to consult the schedule with her, but really to avoid having to acknowledge whoever was coming.

"So, you're leaving Sunday?" she asked, louder than was necessary.

"That was the plan, yes," I replied, trying to stifle the smile at this sudden charade.

"Hmm. Well maybe I could put you down for a reading tomorrow evening then, maybe right after the panel, if that's all right." She looked at me and her gaze snapped to the air over my shoulder, then back to me. "It would be the perfect time, I think. Don't you?"

The urge to laugh was almost painful, and I put a hand over my mouth, watched her lips do a funny dance as she tried not to be infected by the grin.

"I do," I told her in a wobbly voice, and she might have laughed then, had not the object of her dismay stepped close enough for me to smell his aftershave.

"Ms. Vassar?" inquired a soft voice, and we both looked up. The man before us was a tall, anemic-looking sort, his wide expanse of brow peppered with dry skin, sallow cheeks bisected by a bulbous nose that looked like a support group for divorced capillaries. A weak chin hung flaccidly beneath a thin-lipped mouth that was crooked by uncertainty, maybe even embarrassment. What little hair he had was badly dyed and combed back, allowing a pair of large jug-handle ears to dominate his skull. His surprisingly sharp and clear green eyes moved from Audrey's face to mine.

"Hello," he said meekly, and offered his hand, which I shook. It was cold and clammy. He didn't, however, offer his name, but I recognized him as one of the two men who'd been stressing over paperwork at the far end of the bar. "I'm sorry to interrupt, but if I could have a word?" he asked, casting his apologetic glance from me back to Audrey.

"Well, I'm kind of in the middle of something," she said sweetly. "Perhaps later?"

"Oh sure, sure," he said, and nodded furiously. "I really didn't mean to interrupt. It's just my room."

"Your room?" Audrey inquired, and I noticed her hand was still on my knee, then saw our guest notice too, though he tried not to. "What's wrong with it?"

"Well..." He winced, as if he really did not care to be such a bother. "The toilet seems to be broken."

"Oh." Audrey put a shocked hand to her mouth, but there was a smile behind it. "Oh my God, I'm so sorry."

The man smiled. "It's really not a big deal. I shouldn't even have made an issue of it."

"No, no, you're absolutely right to come to me. I'll have a word with the receptionist and get her to send someone up to take care of it as soon as possible. Room 31, isn't it?"

"Yes." He did a kind of half-bow, and flashed a set of perfect teeth at us. "That's really very good of you, and I'm sorry again to have intruded."

"It's no problem," I told him, and Audrey nodded her agreement.

With another of his bows, as if someone had surreptitiously bestowed knighthoods on Audrey and me, the man headed out of the bar. Before the doors swung shut, I saw a young man stop him in the hall beyond and shove a hardcover book and pen in his face.

Audrey sighed and went back to her drink. "That's the third time since he's been here that he's complained. Last time it was that someone seemed to have thrown up in the elevator. Turned out to be a bag of fries someone had stepped on"

"Valid concerns, though."

"And you wonder why I drink."

"He seems harmless enough. Who is he?"

"Maurice Satzenberg."

"Never heard of him."

"You wouldn't have. He writes as Kent Gray."

* * *

I once met Stephen King at a signing (his, not mine) in New York, and his indifference to me might be why I went off his work in later years. It never occurred to me that he might have been jetlagged, or hung over, or just plain tired of scratching his signature out on the thousands of books that were dumped in front of him, or that he only had so much tolerance for star struck fans who seemed to think, as did I, that he owed them a piece of his soul for all their support over the years. At the time, I figured that since I bought, read and enjoyed his books, I deserved some of his time, forgetting that in writing the book, he'd already given it to me, maybe a year or two, or three, and also forgetting that he wasn't just some magical writing machine impervious to the trivial concerns of human beings. I wouldn't realize any of this until later, until I was on the other side of that table, with fewer fans, but as many troubles.

What had taken me by surprise, however, was how he looked in real life. On the back of the book clutched in my feverishly trembling hands—*The Shining*, if I remember correctly—he was dark-haired, heavily bearded, and young. The man hunched over the table in that bookstore was painfully thin, gaunt, and beardless.

There were resemblances sure, but I couldn't tell how many of them were because I was innately aware that they were the same person. Kent Gray looked nothing like the picture I'd seen of him on his website, my Google searches, or on the back of *Cyclopean Heart*. There he'd been heavier, even slightly pudgy, tanned that dubious George Hamilton shade that seems to come from a squeeze-tube rather than the sun, and which emphasized the whiteness of his immaculate teeth. His eyes had been piercing, alight with intelligence and humor. A full head of jet-black hair had been flattened down and coaxed to the sides, parochial style, and his pose, hands clasped around an Annie Proulx novel, had been one of contentment, making him appear as if the photographer had interrupted him while he was busy being perfectly at ease with the world and everything in it.

Only discovering that Gray was actually a blind transvestite midget from Cuba would have shocked me more than the revelation that he was in fact the pitiful-looking and socially inept man who'd just slouched out of the bar.

"You're fucking kidding me."

Audrey, taken aback by the coarse disbelief in my tone, followed my gaze to the closed door, and frowned. "What?"

"That was Kent Gray? The Kent Gray?"

"Yes." A possibility she hadn't considered seemed to dawn on her and she bit her lower lip. "Oh…are you a fan of his? If so, I'm—"

My laughter was like a gunshot that ripped through the ambiance of the bar and made heads turn. Audrey herself jumped and looked around to see how many people had noticed she was sitting with a loon. I raised a hand in apology, and composed myself, but my smile was an indelible one.

"I'm not a fan. No. In fact, I'm as far from being a fan of that man's work as you can probably get."

"Thank God," she said with a shake of her head, and went back to her cigarette.

The glee abated a little when it dawned on me that all along, my envy and burgeoning hatred had been directed, not at the sad sack that had just left my company, but at the words said sad sack had produced, and while his outer shell may have atrophied noticeably, how likely was it that his talent had? There was Kent Gray, and—

"What was his name again? His real name?" I asked Audrey.

"Maurice Satzenberg."

—and Maurice Satzenberg. So which one did I hate? Both, because they were the same guy, or just Gray because that was the persona by which his talent was known? That had to be it, because I certainly couldn't drum up enough animosity for that poor guy I'd just seen asking for his toilet to be fixed. No. I had nothing against Satzenberg, but plenty of ire still left for a guy kids hitchhiked thousands of miles in the cold to see.

"Will you excuse me?"

Audrey seemed to have been daydreaming. Either that or she was suddenly feeling the effects of a vodka tonic she had all but drained. Whatever the case, she took her time answering. "Sure. I'll be here if you need me."

"Thanks." I left her and my beer behind, and headed for the lobby.

* * *

My intention was to corner Gray, and maybe invite him to dinner, or back to the bar so we could talk. I had no idea if he'd go for it, but that was my plan. With any luck, Walt would spot us and remember our deal. To be honest, that didn't matter nearly as much now as it had before I'd met the real Kent Gray, so if Walt didn't show, then to hell with it. I still wanted some alone time with the soft-spoken golem.

But I hadn't even managed to penetrate the crowd between the bar and the lobby before a duo of Asian teens did a double-take in my direction, then hustled to block my path, gibbering at me in Chinese or Japanese. With eerie synchronicity they dropped to the ground the backpacks they'd been hefting on their shoulder and began to rummage through them. At last, they located two copies of *Cutters Inc.* and presented them to me for signing. I obliged, inscribing the first copy to Koshi, the second to Kiro. They nodded their thanks, asked me to pose for a photograph with each of them, then hustled away again on a wave of excited, if unintelligible chatter, bound for the next author on their list. Shortly thereafter, a girl in

Goth clothing swished her way over to me. She couldn't have been more than sixteen but seemed to have more of a knowledge of my books, and in particular the gruesome scenes, than anyone I had yet encountered in my career. She was a pretty thing, at least as much as I could see through the layers of pasty white makeup, and a lot more mature than my estimation of her years suggested she should be.

"You're the only reason I came," she said flatly, and I thanked her, feeling awkward as I did. "I love your words." She regarded me with an innocence that might have given Nabokov an anxiety attack, though I accredited whatever latent sexuality she might be utilizing to a misguided adolescent belief that sleeping with me—weaver of such deliciously evil tales—would escalate her in the eyes of whoever measured her worth as a human being—assuming it wasn't herself.

"Can I email you?" she asked, coquettishly.

"Sure. My email is online at—"

"I have your email," she responded, tonelessly. "I just didn't want to use it until I asked your permission."

"Well now you have."

"Thank you. I just eat this stuff up. Anyone who doesn't is a loser." She leaned in close and kissed my cheek, then, like the very character she had dedicated herself to playing, vanished into the milling crowd, a vampire among aliens.

I shook my head and continued on, stopped intermittently and each time unexpectedly by more readers, many of whom complimented my work with such fervor I couldn't help but be flattered, and encouraged. Their genuine praise almost made me wish I'd bought a cheap laptop so I could get back to work as soon as the evening was through. Despite the signings I'd done over the years in generally low-rent neighborhoods, in squalid stores six months before they went out of business or were burned down, I'd never truly felt the love some people had for my books. Sales figures were one thing. It meant people were buying my books, but none of them had a face, or a voice that whispered to me when the words wouldn't come that I should continue, that they had depleted their stock of Tennant books and wanted more. For the past few years I'd been writing for my agent and my editor, and for myself. I'd found it hard to picture it going further than that. My books were available in most of the chain stores, but Wal-Mart and its like refused to carry them because of the covers, in which invariably a woman's breast or bare ass was shown beneath some kind of a gleaming weapon. Misogyny, remember? And Wal-Mart doesn't want women to stop shopping there because they chanced upon an illustrated tit and a scissors in the book section. Makes me wonder where the women who frequent Barnes & Noble do their grocery shopping.

Suffice it to say, I had all but forgotten about Kent Gray, so elated was I by this newfound love and encouragement, the absence of which might very well have contributed to my inexplicable targeting of the author in the first place. Though I had assumed it wouldn't make a difference, it did appear as if my name as guest of honor had drawn a small cabal of supporters, all of whom came armed with copies both new and old of my titles. With a shit-eating grin I wandered among them, glad to scribble my name on the books, photos, arms, and the single drooping breast that was presented, much to the enjoyment of a crowd of nearby Cylons, who laughed so hard they had to remove their heads to breathe. I shot the breeze with a few horror authors I estimated were not far enough above or below my place on the career ladder for me to feel threatened by or imperious toward them, and so relaxed in their company.

On I went, entertaining and being entertained, feeling the dark cloud inside me dissipate as I navigated the labyrinthine corridors of the hotel, pausing here and there to indulge my own taste for the macabre, admiring the restored copies of much-loved horror classics on DVD (but not the astronomical prices that had been slapped on them), cracking wise with costumed invaders and college kids whose sole concession to the sci-fi masquerade was a rubber probe gun which they delighted in prodding at every female unfortunate enough to pass them. I wandered into a large conference room, populated by B-movie stars of yesteryear, few of whom looked happy to be there sitting beside signed portraits, and sometimes sculptured replicas of their own faces, albeit a few decades younger. One poor guy even had a set of action figures laid out in boxes before him.

His smile looked just as artificial. Despite their chagrin, there were lengthy lines of giddy youths and even some adults, waiting to meet their heroes, every single one of them clutching some piece of merchandise to be personalized by the jaded stars.

Cubicles were set up in the halls between these rooms, offering transformation and transmutation for a couple of dollars a pop, and I waited just long enough to see a ten-year-old child emerge painted green with prosthetic horns sprouting from his head before I moved on, smiling to myself. Now and again, more readers would pass by, then stop and trot back, comparing my face to the mug on the back of my books before asking me to sign them. I started to look forward to such encounters, and of course, that was all it took to ensure they stopped.

A half hour passed, then an hour. The crowd seemed to move like the tide, which I had caught coming in and was now on the way out. The evening was growing older. New guests were starting to arrive. The noise was increasing. I made my way to the bathroom to avoid looking as abandoned as I abruptly felt.

* * *

I hurried into the only unoccupied stall and shut the door, locking it behind me. I had no pressing desire to evacuate my bowels, so I sat down to think for a moment. The process was made difficult by the rustling and grunting sounds filtering through the narrow wall dividing me from the stall on my right. The more I tried to ignore it the worse it got, until I felt like saying something, but as is the case in hotel restrooms, unless wind is being broken, water being run, or torpedoes discharged, it's eerily quiet, and I didn't think I'd been at the convention long enough to have earned the right to piss anyone off, particularly when they were engaged in nothing more sinister than taking a dump.

Only, the sounds from the next stall were not quite like that. The rustling was definitely of some kind of material, maybe being slid on or off, and the grunting was muffled, as if the guy doing it had his mouth full.

A light blinked on over my head and I snorted silent laughter.

It would appear that my noisome throne-mate was busy either relieving the stress of a day spent watching scantily clad alien queens and oiled-up cyber-seductresses strutting their stuff, or he'd managed to coax one of them in there with him. Either way, I wordlessly wished him luck and stood.

The man gurgled. Something thumped hard against the wall, and I paused, stared at it. "Hey buddy, you okay?" I asked, quietly, so as not to arouse the interest of the guy in the stall on the opposite side.

"Fine," came the curt reply, and I nodded, feeling more than a little foolish.

Out I went, and to the sink, where I scrubbed my hands with enough vigor to cleanse myself of the embarrassment. As I rinsed foamy soap from my skin for the third time, I decided that it would be wise to call Kelly soon, just to let her know I was still alive.

Assuming she was there to take the call.

I exited the bathroom, leaving the guy moaning and thumping against the stall door. I resisted the urge to linger in the hall, to see if his appearance would sate my curiosity or provide some clue as to what he'd been up to, then thought better of it and headed for the bar.

The crowd in the lobby had gotten larger and more unruly, no doubt as more alcohol was consumed. The costumes had grown more extravagant, and there was talk of a competition. I recognized a few more of the guests, and some of the writers and industry professionals not on the list who'd shown up because either the convention was local, or they were in town. They stood around, made conspicuous by their lack of antennae, and seemed, like me, to be wondering why on earth they'd come. We exchanged salutes across the heads of a hundred aliens as I made my way into the lounge.

Audrey wasn't there, but Kent Gray was, sitting by himself in what seemed at first glance to be the only area of the bar not dominated by whooping teens and older guys in heavy metal T-shirts who looked like they wished they were ten years younger.

I joined him.

He looked up as I slid into the seat, and offered me an unsteady grin. Clutched in his outstretched hand was an empty glass. By the look on his face, he'd been waiting some time for service, while the barman flirted with a gill-woman six stools up.

"Hey," I called out, loud enough to be heard over the crowd. The barman noticed, frowned in irritation and snapped a dishcloth over his shoulder, then muttered something to his fishy female friend before making his way toward us.

"Yeah?"

I pointed at Kent's empty glass. "This guy's a guest of honor."

The barman didn't look at all impressed. "So?"

"So how fucking long were you planning on making him wait for a drink?"

He appraised me anew. Sure, the guy was ten years younger than me, and at least fifty pounds heavier, most of that extra weight portioned out into muscle, but I didn't give a shit. If he made an issue of it, I could hit him with a chair. Or Kent Gray, who looked even lighter.

But instead of defending his honor for the benefit of his scaly girlfriend, he pursed his lips, and muttered a halfhearted apology.

"Been busy tonight," he said. "Other guy didn't show."

"Beer for me, and . . ?"

"Whiskey. Neat," Kent added, holding up his glass. Then, after the barman moved away in a sulk, he turned to me and smiled.

"Thanks for that, but I didn't mind waiting."

I waved away the gratitude. "They invite you to be a guest, they should treat you like one."

"You've been here before?"

"First time."

"Ah. Well, it's the organizers that invite us, not these poor guys. They don't see anything of the money the Aurora people are pumping into this thing. Just more work."

I pretended to consider this for a moment, then shook my head. "Nope. Can't stretch to sympathy. Sorry."

Amused, he sat back and folded his arms. "I know you from somewhere, don't I?"

"Do you?"

"You're Jason Tennant."

"I am, and you're Kent Gray."

He nodded, a gleam in his tired eyes. "I won't even ask."

"Not a fan, sorry."

He shrugged. "Can't say I blame you. Haven't got much tolerance for my own stuff these days either. I'm becoming the Sidney Sheldon of sex-fi."

I couldn't help but grin at that. "There are worse people to be. Sidney's doing all right for himself."

"I suppose."

As our drinks were delivered, I wondered how best to tell Kent what I'd come here to let him know—that I hated his guts with a passion that frightened me simply because he was the writer I'd been aspiring to be, and didn't know how to be, since childhood. I knew at the core of it that it was insane to blame the guy for something that came naturally to him, and worse to pinpoint his literary prowess as the reason for all my failings, as if the mere presence of his book in my house had acted as a catalyst for my misery. I might as well have asked if he was the one sleeping with my wife; if he had persuaded my father to resent me; if he had whispered in the publishing industry's ear and commanded them to pen me in the stable of mediocrity until I expired from trying to kick free. Yeah, I could see it now, his bushy eyebrows rising further with each lunatic query until they vanished into his thinning hair, and he rolled up after them like a hastily pulled shade. And hell, it wasn't as if there weren't better writers than both of us combined out there.

Jesus, I mean, Michael Chabon, for one, made every writer at this convention—except maybe for George Martin—look like preschoolers trying to figure out if Crayola or snot worked better on paper.

"I read one of your books a few weeks back," he said then, tipping back half the glass of whiskey and smacking his lips in appreciation.

Usually, bar lights complement the drunk and the weary. They're designed to, so you can't look at yourself in the mirror behind the bottles and decide you'd best quit while you're ahead. No, those bar lights, just like readers and wives, are there to convince you you're not half as big a loser as you think you are. But it seemed the wattage hadn't yet been mastered that could chase away the gloominess from Kent Gray's face. Huge swatches of shadow were dug-in beneath his puffy eyes like grease-painted soldiers.

"Yeah?"

"Yeah. Every time I go to a convention, I try to read at least one piece of work by the writers who'll be attending."

"That why you don't go to them often?" I quipped and he made a sound that was half snort, half chuckle.

"I liked it a lot more than I thought I would," he told me. "I don't usually go for the visceral stuff. I find most of it reprehensible, to tell you the truth."

"And mine was different...why?"

"Because it had real people in it. And real people with real fears. They weren't cardboard cutouts waiting for the shredder. I felt for them. Feared for them, and if I'm not mistaken, that's what horror is supposed to do."

"Thanks," I said, rather tonelessly. In truth, I was stunned. Here I was, agonizing over the best way to inform him that I'd hardly grieve if a goodly sized portion of the ceiling came down and stove his skull in, and he was handing out compliments. So, while I wasn't naive enough to dismiss the possibility that he was simply stroking my ever-vulnerable ego, I couldn't deny that he looked too goddamn troubled to lie.

"I got the feeling there was a lot of you in that book," he added, draining his glass.

"Which one?"

He replied without looking at me. "Does it matter?"

I hadn't yet taken a drink from my bottle, but I did now, and raised a finger to get the bartender's attention. Unsurprisingly, he pretended he hadn't noticed, so I rapped a fist on the counter. That he responded to, and promptly refilled Kent's glass.

"If you don't mind my saying so, you don't look particularly thrilled to be here," I told Kent, wishing Audrey were here so I could bum a smoke. I wasn't about to bother anyone else for one.

"I'm just tired, and getting a bit too old for the touring circuit."

"That what this is? Part of a tour?"

"Uh huh." He touched a finger to his chin. "Promoting the latest, though I told my publicist I didn't think it necessary. I'm at that great stage where I think people can find my books on their own."

"Lucky you," I said, wincing inwardly at the bitterness in my tone.

"You'll get there," he told me. "If you quit dancing around the subject you're attempting to study."

I'd been slugging on my bottle. Now I stopped, and slowly lowered it. "What subject?"

He considered his response for a moment, like a wine he wasn't quite sure he liked, then turned and looked at me, those sunken eyes locked on mine. "The one you think you're already writing about. The same one we all fear: Death. Mortality. Isolation. Fear of being alone. Fear of having to bury our loved ones, and the selfishness of wanting to go before them, despite the terror the mere thought of it instills in us." He tilted his head. "Close?"

I nodded, slowly.

"The bad news is," he said with a sigh. "It doesn't get any easier to write about the closer you get to it. Which is why my next novel isn't going to a popular one."

"Why's that?"

"My agent's not going to know what to do with it. It's more metaphysical and spiritual than sex-fi. There's no sex at all in it actually, aside from a few mentions of what the act of lovemaking means to the spirit."

"Heavy."

"Maybe too much so."

"Why the dramatic change?"

He shrugged. "The last one should be the one you want to be remembered for, I think."

"You're quitting?"

He studied my face for a moment, then finished his drink. "The whole goddamn ball game," he said, then tipped an imaginary hat, and rose.

As I swiveled in my seat, a hundred questions flooded my mind, drowning in a great tidal wave of immediacy the lingering strains of my bitterness and anger. Whoever this man was, he was not Kent Gray, but Maurice Satzenberg, a man afraid of the same things I was, as human and flawed as I was, who didn't consider talent a free pass to anywhere, a man trapped in a machine that forced him to crank out replicas of his work over and over again until even he couldn't bear it. But did that mean his retirement was going to come in the form of a suicide? The enigmatic way in which he'd ended our conversation certainly suggested as much. And though it was none of my business, suddenly I needed it to be, needed to know, because the frightening thought had occurred to me more than once during our brief exchange that I had not been looking at Gray, or Satzenberg after all, but at a tarnished mirror image of myself.

"Wait."

He didn't, and I stood to follow him.

But whatever I might have said to him next was forgotten when the doors exploded inward hard enough to send them smacking against the wall, and Audrey Vassar stumbled into the room screaming.

She was covered in blood.

* * *

This is how I imagine it happened. This is how the movie plays night after night behind my eyes, though I've tried so desperately

164

hard not to keep dreaming my way to that theater, with its dilapidated façade and the posters of *Raw Red Smile: The Motion Picture* pasted all over the place, the edges torn and bleeding red. I'm always alone on that dead, empty street, craning my head back, though I don't want to, to observe the legend on the marquee, the chunky black letters stained and running with the verdigris of night: JASON TENN*ANT*: THE CRACKHEAD'S CHOICE!

I don't make my own way inside, past the lightless ticket booth. I'm just there, seated in the darkened theater, alone, always alone at first, the rows of vacant seats stretching out around me until they're lost in the gloom. The jaundiced lights flicker briefly, sending shadows fleeing into the walls, ducking between the seats, then out, and the dark is suffocating. It lasts forever, but in this dream, forever is a mercy not nearly long enough.

An enormous wrinkled screen glows with the intensity of a freight train's light seen by its victim at the moment of death, and of course, that's exactly what I've been ushered in to see, for the thousandth time, and when at last the credits roll, I should be relieved to realize I'm no longer alone. But I'm not, nor can I turn my head to see if the expression on my dead father's face has changed. I don't need to. In the periphery, he is a charcoal blob, slowly shaking his head.

There is a sudden burst of discordant music. It blares from the speakers set high above our heads and all around us, a torturous sound, like MGM fanfare played in reverse. I want to block my ears, but this is a dream, a nightmare, and in the inevitable, inexorable wasteland of the subconscious, such options are unavailable.

The picture begins.

There I am, a wretched creature in a suit with frayed cuffs, smiling a clumsy smile at a pair of Asian youths as they tell me in a language I don't understand, how much they love my work. I nod, looking pained, as I suspect I always do, even when I'm not aware of it, and they hurry away.

In keeping with the hyperkinetic style that has become so popular in today's movies, mine without reason or apology cuts abruptly and jumpily to a medium shot of me in the hallway, looking lost, looking brave, as if afraid everyone there will discover that I'm a fraud. A comical moment ensues, complete with the Snagglepuss sound effect of scrambling, exit stage left, even as I duck into the bathroom. The camera stays on the bathroom door as it swings shut behind me.

This is where I want it to stay.

But of course, it doesn't.

The next shot is an overhead one, starting from the stall on the far left, floating like a disembodied spirit, looking down on a bald headed man, pants around his ankles, multi-colored pamphlet in hand as he sighs in time with a silent emission of bodily gas. The camera continues, coming to rest over the man in the middle stall.

That's me, in a similar pose as the bald man, but fully dressed and stressed. My hands are in my hair, my head down, feet spread wide apart on the floor. I cut a pathetic figure, mired in self-pity, worried as always about things I can't control. But this dream is the ultimate exercise in loss of control because now I have the benefit of omnipotence, seeing the scene through the vapid, uncaring eye of a movie camera. It may only be based on a true story, but it's close enough and real enough to terrify me.

On the screen, still seen from above, my head turns to the right, and the camera pans accordingly. And I'm looking down on two people standing, crushed into the confines of the cubicle. At first glance, they might be making love, silently if frantically, and I would prefer to think they were. But the camera, still gazing voyeuristically down, begins to zoom in, slowly.

There is a man and a woman.

The man is leaning back against the far wall, his feet on both sides of the toilet, his bare ass pressed against the tank, the flush handle digging into his spine. One foot has somehow pulled free of his pants, but not his underwear, a soiled pair of boxers that hang from his ankle like a manacle. The other foot is still planted in his crumpled up jeans. A lone shoe lies on its side.

A young woman, naked, her long drab dress hanging crooked on a hook on the back of the stall door, appears to have one hand cupped around the man's genitals, the other on the slim paperback novel she is cramming down his throat.

Here is where movie magic compensates for the limitations of reality. The young man is gagging, foamy blood oozing from a mouth stretched impossibly wide. His legs twitch, trying to kick the woman who moves so fluidly and calmly to stand sideways that she must be a ghost. When she leans back, we see the metallic glint of something in the hand she's holding to her victim's crotch. And though the camera resists the urge to reveal the weapon, to cast a dead eye on it, I know what it is because I used it in a scene once.

A scene much like this one. The woman turns the gleaming straight razor so the blade is held vertically down against the seam dividing the man's testicles. His arms are free, and flapping madly, thumping against the sides of the stall, but he dares not use them to defend himself for fear it will cost him his manhood, a strange concern when it's quite obvious the woman intends to kill him anyway.

Only the bottom third of the book can be seen now, the cover bent almost double, and carving a groove in the man's lower lip. His mouth has split at the sides, making him look like The Joker. The woman has one hand on the bottom of the book, palm pressed flat as if she's trying to stuff a letter into an overfull mailbox. The man's throat swells. Blood runs. He gags, convulses, finally forgets the urge to protect his genitalia, and lashes out at the woman.

"Hey buddy, you okay?" a familiar voice asks, muffled by the wall.

The woman glances casually toward it, ducks her chin to affect a more masculine voice and sneers, "Fine." It should not be so easy for her to keep the man from overpowering her, but she manages, occasionally grabbing fistfuls of his T-shirt and forcing him back against the toilet. Tears stream down his face. His struggling subsides. He moans.

There comes the sound of a stall door opening, then closing. The woman withdraws her hand from the book. Glassy relief enters the man's eyes.

A sink runs; stops. The bathroom door opens, squeals shut. The woman curls her free hand into a fist and punches the edge of the book with all her strength before the man can begin to start trying to dislodge it. He jolts, feet scrabbling, and drops, eyes as wide as his mouth as the light in them fails. In falling, he forces his murderer to withdraw the razor. Something falls to the floor with a splat. The man gives one final moan as blood gushes from his groin. His choking dwindles to the sound of a slowing bass beat heard through a wall.

Then he dies.

The woman leans over where he has come to rest, his head reclined, body crumpled on the toilet, knees wedged against the opposite wall.

She inspects her work, brushes sweaty hair away from the man's brow and gently kisses the skin there. Then she dresses, listens at the door, and hurries out. There are splashes of blood on her skin, now hidden by her dress, spots of spittle and vomit on her arms and neck that can be washed away, and anything she misses will go unnoticed by the convention crowd, ten percent of whom are here to celebrate murder.

From there, the moody monochromatic Seven-style sequence ends, and reverts to brightly lit slapstick as we cut to the hall sometime later. A pasty-faced man wearing a bib of his own vomit flails blindly out into the hall and collides with an alarmed, drunk, and slightly repulsed Audrey Vassar. A laugh track rises as Audrey bats at the man, who appears to be speaking in tongues. Behind him, and taking great care to avoid touching the lunatic, another man sidles into the bathroom. He emerges a split-second later, blanched and nodding along to Vomit Man's raving. Audrey brusquely shoves them both aside and enters the restroom.

Extreme close up of Audrey's face in the *Seven* room.

Dissolve to: that same face, her eyes distant, ringed with mascara, her nose red and raw from crying as we pull back to show her sitting on a chair in the lobby, sipping coffee from a cup that trembles in her hand. The crowd of aliens has been beamed elsewhere, replaced by men in very real uniforms, but the siren lights flickering through from outside preserve the otherworldly atmosphere.

Finally, the credits roll.

My father applauds, a long slow hollow sound like blocks of wood being smacked together. The lights come up, and on the screen, that rolling block of white against black ends on a single line:

IN MEMORY OF WALT NEUMANN (1986 - 2004)

And I wake.

* * *

I never saw Kent Gray again. Whether or not he avoided me because of my connection to the murder, I'll never know. It could be that he might have liked to have concluded our conversation, and couldn't wait until the police were done with me, but I doubt it.

He'd said all, if not more, than he'd needed to.

With marked reluctance, the detectives eventually let me go, just as the sun was rising over Baltimore, and I figured I'd be hearing from them again, probably many times, before they were finally satisfied that I hadn't had anything to do with Walt's murder.

Not that I could blame them. For the first time ever, though I'd written about such things before, I fully understood what it felt like to be an innocent man afraid to tell the truth for fear it will condemn him. But I had to. Had I not, it would have only made things worse.

So: *Yes, I gave the guy a ride, and no, I'd never met him before.*

We didn't argue. We got along just fine.

No, I'm not gay.

Yes I gave him that book you pulled from his mouth, and yes I wrote it.

Yes, the title Raw Red Smile *does seem ironic.*

Yes, I wrote a scene like that, only it was the hitchhiker doing the castrating. And no, it didn't happen in a bathroom.

I do understand why you're keeping me here, but I don't know who might have done this, or why.

I already told you, yes I might have been there, in the next stall, when it happened. I didn't know someone was being killed, or I'd hardly have just walked out and not told someone.

Yes, I live in New York and, no; I won't be traveling anywhere else anytime soon. If ever again.

I walked out into the crisp, cool morning air feeling as if I'd been boiled alive. My head hurt, my throat was sore from talking and smoking, my scalp itched, and all I wanted to do was sleep, despite the horrible feeling that it would be some time before I'd be able to do so without thinking about the murder.

Poor Walt. The guy had seemed completely innocuous, maybe a little bit simple after too many years spent puffing on the peace pipe, and although I hadn't known him long, I had a feeling I'd have liked him. But then, how often do we think such pleasant positive things about the dead, knowing we'll never have to follow through on such speculations?

I located my car and sat with the engine off for about an hour, trying to get my brain to deflate enough to consider the nightmarish and frightening implications of the scene I had just walked away from.

My hitchhiker.

My book.

My murder.

I shook my head, feeling as if I'd emerged from the hotel into a world in which everything had been moved three inches away from where it belonged—like when you come home convinced you've been burglarized but can't find anything missing. Someone had put their dirty fingers in my head and I felt as violated as if I'd been raped. Someone had taken my thoughts and used them as a weapon to take the life of someone I knew. I felt corrupt, unclean, covered inside and out with the kind of foulness no amount of showering can wash away. Then I cracked the car door, leaned out and retched.

Once composed, I plucked the phone from the back seat, trying hard not to look at the boxes or think about the books snuggled within, all of which I resolved to burn once I got home.

The phone's LCD display was a view of a dull morning sky full of rain. The battery was dead. Annoyed, but not enough to incite me to violence had I had the energy, I located the charger, hooked it up, and the display glowed green.

Seven missed calls. All of them from Kelly.

I started the car, hit redial, and when my wife answered, I broke down and sobbed into the phone.

* * *

I spent the rest of that weekend in bed but not sleeping. Kelly stayed with me, except to run interference when the reporters called to get my angle on a murder I'd inspired. She was ruthless with them, the hurt in her voice obvious. I should have been comforted by it, but instead it got me wondering whether the pain in her tone was because she felt sorry for me, or because she wasn't yet sure she could live with a man whose very thoughts had been borrowed to kill a human being. Her frequent assurances that I'd had nothing to do with what had happened weighed heavily on me too. I turned to alcohol for solace but found instead a purgatory of uncertainty.

What if I had been more involved than I'd led myself to believe?

What if my mind was the one doing all the protecting, fabricating my presence in the stall next to the one in which Walt had died when in reality I had been in there with him? After all, I had known Walt. It had been my book that had been crammed into his mouth, and the method of his execution had been one summoned from the Stygian

170

depths of my own mind. Who better to have perpetrated such a hideous crime? If this turned out to be the case, then surely my defense would be a simple one: I was jealous and unstable to the point where my consciousness divided, inducing paranoid schizophrenia and psychosis, wherein, unable to bring myself to harm the true focus of my obsession, I'd simply settled for someone who idolized him.

But there are holes in that theory too.

Such as: why couldn't I have killed Kent Gray if indeed I'd awoken with the capability to do so? Yes, I'd met him in a bar surrounded by people, but surely a mind capable of deceiving itself enough to hide an atrocity of such magnitude would have been able to arrange something. I could have followed Gray to his room, strangled him, and left before anyone knew a thing. I could have waited until the weekend was over and tailed him until we got to a remote location. I could have crept into his room while he slept, and smothered him with a pillow.

Sure I could.

But that aside, there was a much more important flaw in the theory, and that was: Why the calling card? Why the methodical straight-from-the-page reenactment? Wouldn't this have the obvious effect of leading the police straight to me, which it had?

A subconscious cry for help, maybe?

No, I couldn't buy it, and not solely because I didn't want to.

It wasn't me. I was a writer, compelled to farm the fertile fields of imagination, a place so far removed from reality, there were no limitations on what could be done there. I could murder to my heart's content, but in the end, outside of that field, murder was just a word.

Until it happened for real.

Scared, and more alone than ever, I test-ran my hypothetical confession on Kelly, which she vehemently rejected, telling me, as I had tried to tell myself, that I was not a murderer, that a deranged fan had been behind the tragedy, and I was not to blame. Though it had been my book, it could have been anyone's book. It was simply coincidence, she said. Anyone capable of taking another person's life and committed to doing it in the style of a scene that had some unimaginable importance to them, would have done it regardless of which book, or which author's work it had come from. If I hadn't written *Raw Red Smile*, it would be some other poor writer's face splashed all over the news.

As the weeks went by, I let her persuade me because I needed her to, then watched her walk out the door, bound for her mother's and some indeterminate amount of time away from me and my increasingly agitated and unstable behavior, which had the ironic effect of working in contrast to her theory.

She wasn't mad, she promised. She wasn't leaving me. She just thought she had done as much as she could for the time being and now I needed some time to figure it out on my own.

Which I took to mean I was being a great spiraling, all-consuming asshole. And I knew I was. I also knew there was nothing I could do to stop it. So I let her go with the promise to collect her when I returned to myself.

Three days after she left, I got two important emails. The first was from Kent Gray, which came as a surprise, though it might have been more of one if I wasn't drunk as a skunk and alternating between laughing at shadows and threatening them. I double-clicked on the virtual envelope and the white space of his message, broken only by a single short paragraph written in Berling Antiqua font, opened up on my screen. It read:

Dear Jason:

I'm sorry about what happened, both the unfortunate incident in the bathroom, and the one earlier in the bar. I assume this unwelcome education will be exorcised in a future work, which I look forward to reading.

Keep writing the good write,
M.S. (Kent Gray)

Cute, I thought, in no mood for his condolences, or sagely advice, and had to resist the urge to finally let him know the feelings and emotions that had led me to that convention, had led me to him, but instead I hit the delete button and watched his words shrink into oblivion.

I poured myself a drink and moved to the other email, which I assumed would either be more of the same, or another reporter, unwilling to quit sniffing until I threw him or her a bone. The email address was kpgravegirl666@hotmail.com. The subject line read, simply, "You."

Intrigued despite myself, I opened it.

On the first pass, the words meant nothing. More idle praise from some faceless fan. Then I read it again, and again, until I was left going over and over the last line of the message and my nose was almost pressed flat against the screen, my eyes seeing nothing but faint black smudges on large snowy plains.

Her name was Karen Pike.

We'd met at the convention.

She lived for my work.

Just ate it up, in fact.

Anyone who doesn't is a loser.

And she'd signed her note: "With raw red smiles, Karen"

* * *

Despite a promising lead from their number one suspect, the investigation into the murder of Walt Neumann's death continued for another eight months before going cold. Karen Pike was questioned, but insufficient evidence meant they couldn't hold her. After all, a sign-off line on an email to her favorite author combined with an appearance at the convention in which a man she didn't know had been murdered were hardly grounds for a conviction. Even I knew that. So in the end I was left with my suspicions, and the terrible knowledge that if I was right, then not only was Karen Pike still out there, but she might also know who had put the police on to her.

On the rare nights that sleep came for me, I dreamed of abandoned theaters in which the movies still played, and Goth girls with black eyes and bleeding grins force-fed me the products of my own twisted imagination.

* * *

Kelly came back eventually, but didn't stay long. She quit her job at the school, and I quit writing.

Then we quit each other.

I never found out if my paranoia about what she'd been doing in my absence had been justified, but the summer after our divorce I drove by her mother's house and saw her on the porch, laughing with some guy I didn't know. He was good looking, the kind that in the more insecure moments of our marriage I'd pictured as the type she should have been with. He could have been a plumber, or some distant relative I'd never met. It could have been her ex for all I know, or just a neighbor, but I'd be lying if I said seeing her with him didn't break my heart.

She left me the house, and everything in it that wasn't hers, which meant she left it empty. I'd always only thought of it as the cathedral—a larger space for me to pace when my imagination demanded it. It had never been a home, not even for Kelly. In December of that year, I sold it and moved to a small apartment back in Brooklyn.

It's not the same, but my first check is still there when I look up, still tacked to the wall.

What you're reading now is the first thing I've written in years, and will probably be the last, inspired by Kent Gray's last words of advice to me, via email, almost fourteen months before he died from a brain tumor. If you're frustrated by questions unanswered, then maybe you can understand a little of what my life to this juncture has been like. Call me self-involved and egotistical, and I won't argue. I am, I *was*, for a while a writer, and so I can claim those negative attributes as a requirement of the job. All that's behind me now, so I guess it's time at last to find out who or what I really am, to attend those midnight premieres with a more open mind and less fear, and to finally ask my father if he's been shaking his head all this time for me, or for himself. To see if he, like Kent Gray, was nothing more than a mirror for my own self-loathing and fear.

I leave you here then, with this account from an unreliable narrator.

It may be nothing more than a mild diversion from the real world for you, but obviously, being its creator, I hope that's not the case.

As the late great Mr. Gray once said, "The last one should be the one you want to be remembered for."

STORY NOTES

(Note: The following notes contain <u>spoilers</u>. Therefore, it is suggested that you read the stories first so I don't ruin things for you...)

THE TENT

For a writer, inspiration can come from anywhere, and often the origins of an idea can be quite unexpected and unusual. In *Nemesis*, the final book in my Timmy Quinn series, it's suggested that there is another dimension from which creativity originates, a kind of Heaven of ideas, and such a notion, while melodramatic, makes a strange kind of sense to those of us who have ever had to answer the dreaded question: "So where do you get your ideas?" and are left shrugging because we don't always know.

If I asked you where you thought the idea for *The Tent* came from, I'd expect you'd assume it came to me on a camping trip or a jaunt through the woods in which the tale is set (I've been to Hocking Hills many times). Or perhaps I was idling in front of the television during a documentary about parasitic marine life. But you'd be wrong.

The idea for *The Tent* came to me during one particular scene in the little known coming-of-age movie about an Irish-American family dealing with an abusive alcoholic patriarch entitled, appropriately enough, *White Irish Drinkers*. In the film, the younger of two brothers resists the lure of alcohol and crime in favor of painting, which he only indulges in the basement of his family's apartment building to keep it out of sight of his drunken, intolerant father. In flashback we are shown scenes from the boy's childhood which show him cowering in a yellow tent during a violent storm. His older brother comforts him as the tent threatens to tear away and the trees cast sinister shadows on the walls around them. The comfort offered by his brother is something he never forgets.

Later, he paints a picture of the storm-wracked woods from a canted bird's-eye viewpoint. The woods are monochrome, the tent a glowing yellow, indicating its significance in the boy's life, a bright spot in an otherwise mundane and turbulent life. The tent is something he recollects often as his older brother drifts further into a life of crime.

It was the painting that hit me between the eyes and led me to pause the movie and pace for a half-hour, my mind buzzing with the sudden idea of a tent designed to lure to itself lost travelers. The nature of such a thing followed soon after when I thought of lantern fish and their similar method of attracting prey in the dark.

In the weeks that followed, I let the idea coalesce, but when I finally sat down to write it, the words were slow in coming. Initially the idea was to have two brothers hiking in the mountains of Ireland (something I had done with my own brother a few years before), until I realized neither the characters nor the setting was right for this particular tale. So I let it sit and wrote a number of other things, until again, inspiration came and showed me a family, their bond sundered by the various weaknesses of the husband, lost in a storm after losing their camp. The tension would be fun to explore, thought I, with the creature taking a backseat to the equal horror of watching love and mutual respect die a slow and painful, not to mention inevitable, death.

With the correct cocktail of ingredients, I finally had my story. Now you have it too.

I should note that since *The Tent* was released in digital form, the response has been amazing, and I've received enough requests to expand it into novel form that I am giving it serious consideration. After all, it does, like so many of my stories, leave you kinda hanging at the end, and I must admit it would be fun to take my little tent-monster to the big city (kind of like a really screwed up version of *Home Alone 2*.)

<u>YOU IN?</u>

In 2005, Berkley Books released the Abbadon Inn series: three novels centered around a haunted inn in Cape May, New Jersey: *Twisted Branch*, *Dark Whispers*, and *Drowned Night*. The books were written by "Chris Blaine", a pseudonymous banner for the series (the books were actually written by genre stalwarts Elizabeth Massie, Craig Shaw Gardner, and Matthew Costello.) I was a big fan of the series and with Elizabeth's help, went about proposing an idea to the editor for book number four. With the series bible in hand, I conjured up a World War II-era atrocity that, with the hotel as the beacon, imposes its ghosts upon the town. I wrote a prologue featuring poor Peter Haskins as the night security guard who is the first to realize that the inn is not dead, only sleeping, after his presence there awakens it.

Unfortunately, the series was discontinued soon after that (not an attempt to escape having to publish me, I hope) and I shelved my proposal.

Then, two years later, Roy Robbins at Bad Moon Books asked me if I had any unpublished work he could take a look at for his catalogue. At the time, I thought I didn't, and told him as much, only to stumble across the Abbadon file on my computer while doing some spring cleaning. I read it, liked it, removed all references to Cape May and Abbadon, and did some extensive rewriting to make it work as a standalone short story. Whether or not I was entirely successful in this endeavor is of course debatable, and entirely up to you to decide, but I admit I'm quite fond of the atmosphere at play in the story. I'm a sucker for Gothic Victorian and Italianate houses, and to date, every time I see one, it calls to mind *You In?*

It's also the kind of house I intend to buy if I ever hit the big time.

You are, of course, all invited to the housewarming.

As long as you promise not to wake the ghosts.

SELDOM SEEN IN AUGUST

Near the first house I lived in when I moved to the States, there was a road called Seldom Seen. I passed it almost daily and found it such an unusual and enigmatic name for a street it was difficult to resist writing about it. But like so many other ideas, it needed time to simmer before it was ready for the page. When that day eventually came, a few years later, I had moved to a place in the city, and had just been invited to submit a story to Keith Minnion's wonderful, and unfortunately short-lived publishing house, White Noise Press.

I was ten pages into the story before I realized I was incorporating science fiction into the proceedings and that gave me pause. I don't belong or know my way around science fiction, so I was intimidated. Ultimately though, I decided that if the story insisted on going in that direction, all I could do was follow and hope for the best. I'm quite fond of the result, despite it being simply a different, more modern slant on the hoary old ghost story. I also like that the protagonist/antagonist Wade Crawford is a complete asshole, not without an ounce of humanity, but close. Bad guys are so much fun to write. And I like the fact that from the outset, you and I both know he's going to get what's coming to him.

MIDLISTERS

As I said in my story notes for the first entry in this collection, *The Tent*, inspiration often comes from the oddest of places. But it can also come from a very obvious, very ordinary place. In the case of *Midlisters*—easily the story I get asked about most often—all I really had to do for this one was to look at writers and the things that make us tick: the insecurities, the stress, the envy. When people treat writers as lazy louts who sit around throwing make-believe nonsense onto the page, an assumption usually followed by the suggestion that they get "a real job" I want to rip off their faces and sew them to a football (or maybe just disabuse them of the notion, whichever seems less likely to get me arrested at the time). I've worked as a waiter, cartographer, fraud investigator, security guard, warehouse assembly line worker, barman, teacher, and a host of other jobs, and none of them were harder jobs than this one. Don't get me wrong, I love it to death. It's my dream job, and I wouldn't quit it for anything. But I've never had a job that requires such hostile hours (even when you're not writing, you're thinking about writing, agonizing over plot points, etc, considering other stories), leaves you so open to as much praise as criticism, exhausts you to the point of illness, and requires you to feed a compulsion 24/7 that is worse and more potent than any drug. It requires us to make sacrifices we are not always aware we're making. It makes us moody and unsociable. Every word you make available to a reader is like holding out your hand to a room full of people as well-versed in the art of mutilation as they are in kindness. You put yourself out there, your intimate thoughts, fears, horrors, and needs, and readers will do with them as they will. You watch other writers race ahead of you in the success game and you try to not let it get to you.

But the truth is, on bad days, sometimes it does.

Midlisters is the story of that day, though for Jason, *every* day is a bad day.

I've been asked endlessly if *I* am Jason Tennant. I am, only insofar as Jason is every writer. I don't have any jealousy or animosity toward any one writer, though I dislike one or two of them based on my personal encounters with them. That's natural though. We're still people and not everyone connects. And some people are just assholes. I'm perfectly capable of being one myself. (Ask anyone who's met me on one of *my* bad days.)

Writing's a tough game on an uneven playing field, and with the advent of digital publishing, it's no longer a specialty, or something that distinguishes you from anyone else. Now everybody's a writer. Had I written *Midlisters* in the wake of the digital explosion, perhaps Jason might have been heartened at having a new avenue for his work (like I am), or perhaps he'd have thrown himself off a bridge at the sight of lesser writers rushing up the Kindle charts. I assume the latter might be the case. I created Jason as weak, vulnerable, as unsure of his talent as he is sure of Kent Gray's. Most writers possess this kind of insecurity, and it occurred to me that while novelist protagonists are a dime a dozen, I hadn't read a story that really dug into the guts of the monsters we can be, the monsters the pursuit of validation, acceptance, and creation can make of us.

Midlisters is a story about our ugliness as artists. Most of the writers I heard from after it was released recognized something of themselves in poor Mr. Tennant. Most readers assumed it was autobiographical. Some of the background stuff is, particularly about the struggle to get published in the first place. The paltry check did hang on my office wall for a long time (it ended up getting lost in the move), and I did live in a crappy little apartment and drink too much when I got my first acceptance. And the convention Jason attends is pretty much based on my first trip to Horrorfind. There was no Audrey, no Kent Grey, though I did meet a few writers who had aged so much since the last jacket photo I saw of them, they were virtually unrecognizable. And many of the B-movie celebrities did look pissed off and bored, but that's pretty much a common sight to any horror convention-goer.

And of course, there was no murder.

Because murder's just a word.

Until it happens for real.

- Kealan Patrick Burke
May 2013

ABOUT THE AUTHOR

Born and raised in Dungarvan, Ireland, Kealan Patrick Burke is the Bram Stoker Award-winning author of five novels (Master of the Moors, Currency of Souls, Kin, The Living, and Nemesis: The Death of Timmy Quinn), over a hundred short stories, three collections (Ravenous Ghosts, The Number 121 to Pennsylvania & Others, and Theater Macabre), and editor of four acclaimed anthologies (Taverns of the Dead, Quietly Now: A Tribute to Charles L. Grant, Brimstone Turnpike, and Tales from the Gorezone, proceeds from which were donated to children's charity PROTECT.)

Kealan has worked as a waiter, a drama teacher, a mapmaker, a security guard, an assembly-line worker at Apple Computers, a salesman (for a day), a bartender, landscape gardener, vocalist in a grunge band, and, most recently, a fraud investigator. He also played the male lead in Slime City Massacre, director Gregory Lamberson's sequel to his cult B-movie classic Slime City, alongside scream queens Debbie Rochon and Brooke Lewis.

When not writing, Kealan designs covers for print and digital books through his company Elderlemon Design. To date he has designed covers for books by Richard Laymon, Brian Keene, Scott Nicholson, Bentley Little, William Schoell, and Hugh Howey, to name a few.

In what little free time remains, Kealan is a voracious reader, movie buff, videogamer (Xbox), and road-trip enthusiast.

WWW.KEALANPATRICKBURKE.COM

Made in the USA
Las Vegas, NV
05 January 2024

83973317R00111